AWAKENING

One woman's journey to Independence

J.L. COATES

BOOKS BY THE AUTHOR

Non Fiction by Judith Coates

Be Who You Be

Let your Light shine

Fiction by J. L. Coates

The Enlightenment Series

Second Chances

Library and Archives Canada Cataloguing in Publication

J.L. Coates

ISBN: 978-0-9880735-2-4

Printed in USA by Createspace
Cover from Createspace archives

iv

DEDICATION

This is book is dedicated to each reader who, as a single parent, serves as mother and father to their children.

I admire you.

CONTENTS

ACKNOWLEDGMENTS

Once again I thank Dianne Tchie for editing this novel, Clarice Nelson for taking the time to read the final draft, and to Shirley Connolley, my most ardent supporter. Without you, this would not be possible. This is a work of fiction, and is based entirely upon my over active imagination.

Courage does not always roar

Courage is the quiet voice, at the end of the day,

which says" I will try again tomorrow."

Deborah Collins

This is not the life I wanted.

CHAPTER ONE

Alicia Browning paced restlessly back and forth along the veranda of their newly renovated farm house. The night was calm. Stopping every once in a while, she stared at the top of the hill searching for the lights of Moe's truck as he came around the curve and started down, She strained to hear the sound of his Jake brake gearing the truck down as he neared home. There was no sound. Something was definitely wrong.

From the time she awakened this morning she had an uneasy feeling, a sense of foreboding. But try as she might, she couldn't pin point why.

Alicia's husband Moe was a long distance truck driver, so it wasn't unusual for him to get home later than he thought, but this time felt different. *"He should have been home yesterday. Why hasn't he called?"* she whispered into the night air,*" he always calls when he gets close to home."*

They had fought bitterly the day he left on this trip. Maybe that was why she felt uneasy, but it seemed like that was all they had been doing lately. This time it was her fault. She knew Moe was under a lot of stress, and maybe she shouldn't have been so sarcastic when she answered his questions. She didn't mean to be, but the words came out that way. As usual, one word led to another until he had walked out, slamming the screen door behind him.

As he climbed into his truck she supressed the

urge to run behind him and apologize. There would be time for that when he got home and they had cooled down.

She went upstairs to bed but tossed and turned for what felt like hours. She had barely dozed off when the ringing telephone beside her bed jolted her awake. *"Why would Moe be phoning this time of the night? It's 3 a.m. and I have had less than two hours sleep. He knows I have to get up early with the kids."*

"Hello," she answered sleepily,

"Mrs. Alicia Browning?"

"Yes."

"Mrs. Alicia Browning of Millarville?"

"Yes." By now Alicia was wide awake and sitting on the edge of the bed. Her hands were shaking. The lump of dread she had fighting all day settled into the pit of her stomach. "Has something happened to Moe? Has there been an accident?"

"No accident ma'am, but there is a problem. This is trooper John Miler of the Border Crossing Patrol. Your husband, Maurice Browning has been arrested for transporting drugs across the border from Mexico."

"Mexico? You must be mistaken," she said incredulously. "He doesn't go to Mexico; he is on his way home from Greensboro."

"Afraid not ma'am, we have him here in custody. As a courtesy we are notifying you as he requested. Later this morning we will be moving him to a Federal facility while his case is being investigated."

Alicia was stunned. *"What in the hell was going on?"* she asked herself.

"Can I talk to him?"

"No ma'am. Once he has been processed we will give him an opportunity to phone you and a lawyer. We expect this to be completed around noon our time."

"I don't understand what this is all about?"

"Like I said ma'am, he is under arrest for transporting drugs into the country from Mexico. Have a good day."

The phone went dead. Alicia continued sitting on the edge of her bed staring at the instrument in her hand. Feeling devastated she placed the receiver back into its cradle.

"What just happened?" she muttered. *"Moe Browning, what have you gone and done this time? I thought you were past the age of getting into trouble."*

Alicia shook her head. He had changed so much during the past three years that she didn't know what to expect anymore. He was secretive, erratic and unpredictable.

She had considered a lot of things including the fact that he had a girlfriend tucked away some place, but drugs? He despised them, and everything they stood for. They were the last thing he would get mixed up with.

Putting on her pink fluffy housecoat and slippers she crept quietly down the stairs careful not to wake up the children. It was too early for them to be up yet. Besides, she didn't want to have to cope with tired cranky children today on top of trying to find out what was going on. She had tried but it was impossible to go back to sleep. She needed Moe to tell her this was a stupid mistake.

Alicia crept into the kitchen, turned on one of the lights under the cupboard, and made a pot of coffee. The dim light filled the kitchen with a soft glow as she sat listening to the coffee dripping into the pot.

"This is all wrong. I know for a fact that Moe wouldn't jeopardize his job and family this way. Moe Browning, you better have a good explanation for this when you get home."

The nagging little voice in the back of her mind insisted on telling her that everything Moe had done over the past two years was beginning to make sense, but why? *"We were happy. Sure at times we had money problems, but didn't everyone at one time or another? We always managed to get through somehow. The biggest problem was that Moe was never satisfied. He always wanted more or bigger. It seemed as though he had to prove to everyone around him that he was as good as they were.*

Alicia felt secure in her own world. She had all of the things she had dreamt about and wanted since she was a foster kid moving from one home to the other; a husband who loved her, three beautiful children and a decent roof over her head.

Lately though she had the feeling that her world was too good to be true. Over the past few months, her deep feelings of insecurity had started to surface again. She tried desperately to ignore the questions that were constantly gnawing at her all the time. Why was Moe late? Where did he go on his trips? Where had his new found money come from?

She replayed the phone call in her mind. *"No,"* she said. *"Moe wouldn't do that to us. He assured me that he stopped making those special deliveries for Stan, the ones his boss Tuk didn't know about. If he knew drugs were involved he would have stopped right away. This whole idea was crazy."*

CHAPTER TWO

Her mind drifted back to the first time she had met Moe. A product of the social welfare system, Alicia had bounced between foster homes from the time she was six years old. Sometimes she tried to remember what her mother used to look like, but couldn't any more. She didn't know who or where her father was.

She still remembered the day her mother taking her to Auntie Rosie's, who was going to babysit her for the afternoon. Three days later, when her mother hadn't come to pick her up, Auntie Rosie had called Social Services. They came that afternoon, took her away and she never saw either of them again.

When she was first married she had tried to find her birth mother, but she seemed to have disappeared off the face of the earth. Finally she gave up.

At sixteen, she moved to Millarville to begin living with the Clarkes, an older couple who specifically took in teens entering high school. They insisted upon good grades and good attendance from their charges, many of whom went on to graduate and have successful lives and careers.

Lucy, one of Alicia's Social workers, had gone to great lengths to get her placed there. Alicia was small and shy for her age, but a very good student. Somehow Lucy knew she would thrive in that environment, and she had. Mrs. Clarke became the mother Alicia never had.

Alicia smiled as she remembered meeting Moe at her first school dance. She didn't want to go but Mrs.

Clarke insisted.

"This is a good way to meet people Alicia," Mrs. Clarke remarked as she dropped her off in front of the school doors. "Call when you are ready to come home and I will come and pick you up."

Bravely she had walked through the front doors, but the closer she came to the gymnasium the more nervous she became. She recalled standing at the gym door, listening to the music, afraid to venture in.

"You that new kid, that foster kid at Mrs. Clarkes?" a deep voice behind her said.

"Yes," she replied, her face turning a bright red.

"My name is Moe Browning. What's yours?"

"Alicia"

"Well Alicia with no last name. Wanna dance?

"I don't know how, I never learned."

"Come on, I'll show you, it's easy. All you have to do is move your feet like this" he gestured, demonstrating a few steps.

The evening was magical. Patiently Moe had taught her a few easy steps, and then danced with her for the rest of the evening. That was the first time in her life she remembered having fun.

When the dance ended he had waited with her until Mrs. Clarke arrived to pick her up.

"Did you have a good time Alicia?" she inquired. "Was that Moe Browning waiting with you?"

"Mrs. Clarke, I had the best time of my whole life," she replied.

Only a couple of inches taller than her, Moe wasn't handsome by any standard. He had large brown eyes, dark brown hair and a smile that lit up his face. His well-worn clothes hung from his skinny frame, and he seemed to be all arms and legs. After that evening they were inseparable.

Even now Moe was her prince charming, her knight in shining armour. He made her feel like a queen, and encouraged her to forget where she had come from. Eleven years later she loved him as much as she did the first day they met.

Mr. And Mrs. Clarke hadn't approved of Moe, said he was too wild, but Alicia didn't agree with them. They didn't know him like she did. He was warm, funny and in love with her.

By the time she reached grade twelve Mr. Clarke was dying from liver cancer. At one point Mrs. Clarke had suggested that she would be better off moving to a different foster home. She remembered how she had begged to stay until she graduated She promised to keep her grades up, which she did. As well, she worked at the five and dime store after school for extra money. It had taken a lot of talking, but finally Mrs. Clarke relented and agreed to let her stay.

Another dream Alicia had was to just once in her life wear a beautiful dress, like the ones the women wore in the movies. Graduating from high school was the perfect occasion. Mrs. Clarke didn't have any extra money to help her; in fact she was barely making ends meet even with Alicia paying her room and board. Mr. Clarke's medication was very expensive, and his insurance didn't cover it all.

Alicia smiled as she recalled the day she spotted the perfect dress in the window of the local dress shop. The pale silver dress had reminded her of the dresses Grecian goddesses wore in the movies. The plunging V-neckline and wide straps were embellished with silver sequins. In the centre of the bodice was a rose shaped medallion outlined in pale pink sequins. A wide silver and pink sequined band circled the empire waist. The shimmery, softly pleated material had puddled to the floor leaving only the tips of her shoes visible. When she finally built up enough courage to try the dress on it fit perfectly. She remembered feeling like Cinderella as the material shaped itself around her small frame, the shimmery material sparkling like stars in the sky. The dress cost two hundred dollars. It was far more than she could afford but she was determined to have it. She had the shop owner put the dress on lay-away.

She worked two jobs to pay for that dress, her regular job at the five and dime, the other as a waitress at the Stop N Go truck stop. At the end of each week she took her tips and put that money toward the cost of the dress. The nights she worked late Moe picked her up and drove her home.

Moe proposed to her the Christmas she turned eighteen, and she said yes. Everything she had ever dreamed of having in her life was coming true. He had bought her a heart shaped ring with a tiny diamond in the centre. She still wore it on a golden chain around her neck. Years later he surprised her with a bigger, more expensive ring, but the first one meant more.

Soon after they became engaged, their relationship became more intimate. In their minds they were committed to each other, and were planning to get married in June the following year. They tried to be careful, but by the first of May Alicia realized she was pregnant.

She would never forget that night she told him. They were sitting in his car in front of Mrs. Clarke's house. Once again, she remembered the fear and anguish she felt as she struggled to find the right words. She was convinced that after she told him Moe would want nothing more to do with her.

"Moe, I need to tell you something" she babbled as she huddled in the corner of the front seat. She wrapped her arms around herself as protection from the words she knew were coming. "I am pregnant," she blurted out.

"Are you sure Alicia? Could this be a mistake?"

"No. I've already missed two periods. There is no mistake. Moe, I am sorry. I never meant for this to happen."

He had sat there quietly, staring out the windshield, and then started to laugh. "Well, I guess baby girl we are going to be getting married sooner than we planned."

"I promised Mrs. Clarke I would finish school and graduate. They have been very good to me. I can't let them down. My grad dress is almost paid for, and I can't afford a wedding dress too. They will be so disappointed in me. I don't know what to do."

"Alicia, everything will be fine." he assured her. "We will figure this out. Imagine me being a father? Wow! I have always wanted a big family with a dozen kids running around."

"Really?"

"Yes really. Alicia, I love you, and I am glad you are going to be the mother of my children. I need you in my life," he said pulling her into his arms.

Together they had gone to Mr. and Mrs. Clarke and told them about the baby. Of course they weren't happy, but wished them well.

Two weeks later, the day after their high school graduation, they were married by a Justice of the Peace. She wore her graduation dress, Mrs. Clarke was her bridesmaid.

They moved into one of Mrs. Kelley's many rental houses, the purple one. All of her houses were painted strange colours. They had a bedroom, tiny bathroom, and a room that served as the kitchen and living room. For the first three months they slept on a mattress on the floor. Weekends they shopped at garage sales and thrift stores to buy furniture for them, and for the baby. They didn't have much, but they were happy.

At night they would lie side by side talking into the wee small hours of the morning. Moe would talk about having it all – his own acreage so he could have horses, buying a Harley Davidson motorcycle, a nice home, and all the things he wanted to give his family. Alicia was content to listen. She already had everything she wanted.

Randy was born five months after they were married. Erin came along when Randy was two, and little Samantha two years after that. Sam had just started kindergarten. Somehow it didn't seem possible for her to be that old already.

The first few years had been hard. Their rent was usually late, and, at times, there was barely enough food in the house to feed themselves and the kids. At first, Moe had drifted from job to job, never quite finding the one he wanted. She smiled to herself. They had been so much in love, and that was what had carried them through the tough times.

Finally he found a full time job with Bill Tucker, the owner of Tucker and Sons Trucking. Tuk, as he was called, often referred to Moe as his son from another mother. Although they were not related, most people assumed that Moe was one of Tuk's boys.

Randy was Moe's pride and joy. He would take him to ride along in the truck for hours. He was determined to act like the father he had never had, and give his son the best of everything.

Life got a little easier after Moe began working for Tuk. She was still angry about the day he had come home and announced "I bought my own truck." Tuk had talked him into it, and agreed to finance him. The two of them had been truck shopping that afternoon and bought a silver and gray 1995 Western Star. They also worked out a deal. Moe would continue working for Tuk as an owner/operator. In turn Tuk would take the payments, insurance and fuel off his pay cheques.

She remembered confronting him "take the truck back. If you are going to make a decision like this you had better to talk it over with me first."

Wearing that funny little grin of his, he had kissed her on the tip of her nose and walked away.

Of course she had backed down, but they continued to struggle. In the winter, when hauling in the oil patch was the busiest, they had lots of money. Moe would spend freely, buying anything he wanted. He didn't believe in saving for another day.

In the spring and fall, when there was little work, Alicia had often felt desperate trying to keep the bills paid, When Sam was three she had gone to work part time as a Teacher's Aide at the local elementary school. Moe wasn't happy about her going to work, but the money she made paid for the groceries when Moe wasn't busy.

After Tuk had been awarded a contract for long distance hauling Moe bought a thirty foot reefer van. He loved the long distance hauling. He kept telling her "this was is my one opportunity to satisfy my wander lust, see more of the country, and get paid at the same time." Their financial situation improved. Even though Moe spent his money as fast as he could make it, Alicia managed to save a little each month for a down payment on a house. Still renting from Mrs. Kelly, they had moved to a larger three bedroom home, but she yearned for a home to call their own.

Their first car was a five year old, second hand Burgundy coloured Suburban. It was rusting out on the wheel wells and had a broken tail light, but was mechanically sound. The original dents and scrapes still showed, and she had added one or two herself while learning how to drive.

One summer they had splurged and bought a second hand travel trailer. The first three years they had gone camping for two weeks every summer, and every other opportunity they could find. Moe had always made a point of taking time off to be with his family. The last two years the trailer had sat in the yard unused. She loved that trailer and missed the many good times they enjoyed.

Each spring she cleaned and stocked it with basic supplies, hoping that they would get away during the summer, but so far each fall she had brought the supplies into the house and used them In fact, she had once again cleaned and stocked the shelves a few weeks ago hoping for a few camping trips. That definitely was out of the question now.

When the kids were small and Moe was home, they would pile into the suburban and go for a drive in the evenings. Usually the kids fell asleep, and then she would put her head on Moe's shoulder, and they would talk like they had when they were first married.

Each time they drove past the Gates' acreage he would tell her, "someday I am going to own that place. You wait and see."

Alicia thought to herself, *"That's Moe's biggest downfall. He wants everything right now. He isn't prepared to work and save for what he wants. Somehow he always manages to be part of one get rich scheme after the other."*

Money continued to be a problem between them. Over the years little had changed, he continued to spend, and she had to find a way to make all of the payments.

Alicia got up from the table and poured herself a

cup of coffee. It was still too early to wake the children for school. Wiping tears from her eyes, she wondered how she was going to explain to them that their dad was in jail and the reason why.

She thought back to when Moe and their idyllic life begun to change. Everything started that day, two years ago, when he rode into the yard on a brand new Harley Davidson motorcycle

She had watched him get off the bike and walk around it, wiping imaginary spots off with his hand. Outraged she had charged out of the back door of the house and confronted him. Slowly she replayed the scene in her mind.

"Hey baby girl, will you look at this," he said exuberantly, "Isn't she a beauty?"

"Moe, where did you get this? We can't afford to pay for it."

"Don't worry your pretty little head. It's paid for, free and clear."

"What do you mean paid for? We don't have that kind of money."

"Remember my investment with Parker Johnson? Well, it paid off big today. I got a sweet deal on this bike, only five thousand cash."

"Five thousand dollars? You spent five thousand on a motorcycle when I don't know how I am going to pay the rent next week. Randy and Erin both need to go to the dentist. You should have thought of that first. Take that thing back right now and get your money back. We have better uses for it."

"I ain't taking it back Alicia. This is bought and paid for, and has nothing to do with you."

"Moe please, you don't know how to ride a motorcycle. The last thing I need is for you to fall off and kill yourself."

"Get off my back. All you ever do is nag about money. No matter how much I bring into this house, it is never enough."

She stood there glaring at him, hands on her hips as if to say, who do you think you are?

"I've had enough of your crap Alicia." he declared putting on his helmet, and getting back on the motorcycle. "I'll be home when I get here," and sped out of the yard.

She remembered lying awake for hours worrying until she heard the bike come into the yard. When Moe finally came to bed she had turned her back to him pretending to be asleep.

Four months later Moe came into the house very excited. "Alicia, Randy Erin, Sam get into the suburban, we're going for a drive."

"Moe, it's time for the kids to go to bed. Can't this wait? They have school tomorrow."

"Never mind baby girl. I have something to show you. Come on kids, hurry up."

Once they were all settled in the old suburban Moe drove out of town to the Gates' place. Instead of stopping on top of the hill as he usually did, he drove into the yard and parked in front of the house.

"Moe, what are you doing? This is private property," she said.

"Not any more. This is ours, I bought it today."

Reaching into his pocket he pulled out a rumpled sheath of papers and handed them to her. "That there is the title baby girl. This place is ours. Hey kids, you can get out and look around if you want."

The kids and Moe got out of the suburban. In shock, Alicia stayed in the vehicle glancing through the papers he had given her, noting that he had paid one hundred and fifty thousand dollars, and for what? The old house was desperately in need of repairs, the lawn was completely overgrown and the white rail fence behind the house was broken. It was going to cost a fortune to fix this place up, and that was money they didn't have. Even now she remembered the sick feeling in her stomach. She had no idea where the money to buy this place had come from.

Moe and the children talked excitedly all the way home. They were making plans about all of the things they were going to do and have once they moved. Alicia was quiet. After the kids were in bed and asleep she walked over to where Moe was watching television, and stood beside his chair.

"Where did this money come from?" she asked, waving the title in the air.

"Don't start Alicia."

"I want to know. Is this another investment with Parker Johnson that paid off big?' she said, her voice dripping with sarcasm.

"Look, don't worry your pretty little head. Everything is cool."

"It is not cool. I demand that you tell me"

Moe looked at her and began yelling angrily "Same old thing. I do something good for you, and then you have to spoil my fun with your bitching and carrying on. Never mind where the money came from. It's none of your business. Now leave it at that." Picking up the remote for the television   he flicked to another channel.

Even now Alicia could feel the sharpness of his rebuke. He never talked to her in that tone of voice. After that evening Moe began pulling away from her and the kids. When his cell phone rang he would go outside so she couldn't hear what he was saying. He also insisted that neither she nor the kids were to answer his cell phone.

Randy noticed the changes more than she or the girls. He and his dad did everything together, but now Moe either ignored or hollered at him.

One Saturday morning, while walking past Randy's room, she heard him crying. Peeking in, she saw him lying face down on the bed, sobbing into his pillow.

"Randy, what's wrong?" she asked sitting down beside him.

"It's dad." he muttered.

"Tell me what happened" she said, gathering him into her arms. He liked to pretend he was too big for cuddling, but today he was open to her embrace.

"I asked him to drive me into town so I could play video games with Toby. He swore, then yelled "can't you see I am busy. Go ask your mother." Mom we used to do thing together all the time, now all he does is yell. What did I do to make him so mad at me?"

"Honey, you haven't done anything. Dad is just tired. I'm going into town later to get groceries; I'll take you to Toby's then. Come on down stairs when you have stopped crying. There is no use you sitting up here alone. You can come help me make some cookies for your lunch next week."

Alicia was at a loss for words. Moe was getting crankier and more miserable with all of them. Each time he returned from one of his trips he retreated into the green Quonset and stayed there for hours. He came to bed when she was sleep, and got up before she awoke. Some nights he didn't come to bed at all, he sat in front of the television sleeping in his chair, cell phone in his hand.

An hour later Moe had come into the kitchen and went straight to the refrigerator. Taking out a can of beer he sat down at the kitchen table.

"Moe, why couldn't you have taken Randy into town? All he wanted to do was spend a little time with you."

Moe was silent.

"He thinks he has done something to make you mad at him." she continued.

"Can't the kid see I'm busy? I've got important things going on and can't be running him into town every time he decides he needs to go. Spoiled brat, that's what he is. That's your fault you know, you cater to every whim of those kids."

Alicia recalled how she stood there looking at him wondering what was going on.

After a while, Randy stopped asking his dad to do anything for him. An invisible barrier arose between the two of them, and nothing Alicia said or did made the situation any better

They had always led a quiet life, but over the last few months that had changed too. Lately Moe had begun inviting his new friends over every weekend to party. There was always lots of food and beer. They made her and the children feel uncomfortable. They were polite, well behaved, but she didn't trust them. She had wondered if Moe needed people around him so he wouldn't have to be alone with her.

More than once she had watched him pull a handful of bills out of his pocket and give them to someone. She doubted that he would get any of the money back. When she had mentioned this to him he laughed, and said it didn't matter, there was lots more where that came from, but when she pressed him for more information, he refused to tell her.

CHAPTER THREE

Alicia looked around her home. It was perfect. Moe had spent a fortune renovating this old farm house. She had to agree with Moe when he said this was a beautiful piece of land to live on. When they first looked at the old farm house they saw that structurally it was in good shape, but needed a lot of work. The roof was partially caved in, most of the windows were broken, and somebody had punched holes in the walls. The contractor Moe hired gutted the inside, taking out most of the interior walls and windows as well as saving and refinishing the original hardwood floor. In actuality, the money would have been better spent building a new house and tearing this one down, but now she was glad she listened to Moe.

The upstairs was converted to four bedrooms and a bathroom. Each of the children had a small cozy bedroom; she and Moe had a much larger room. The carpenter had taken out the small windows and installed glass French doors in their bedroom and added a small deck. When Moe was away, and the children were in bed, she spent many evenings out there. She liked being able to see miles and watching the sunset.

The old rickety stairs were replaced with a graceful curved staircase; the steps from the landing branching into two different rooms. One of them descended into the living room, the other into the family room.

The large family room was her favourite. The carpenter rebuilt the stone fireplace along one wall, and the large windows along another let in the morning sun. This room, always a bit untidy, was where she and the children spent most of their time. Moe had put in a forty-two inch television so they could watch TV and a smaller set so the kids could play their video games.

The kitchen and dining room were now one room with new cupboards and appliances. A patio door opened onto the veranda, which extended around three sides of the house. There was a patio table and chairs outside the door, and when it was hot, she and the children often ate out there. Dozens of flower pots in brilliant hues of red, pink and mauve hung from the veranda roof. By the front door there was a wicker rocking chair and a "Welcome" sign. The back door opened into a large sunlit room which contained the washer and dryer, and was connected to the full bathroom off the family room.

Moe had built a rope swing for the kids in the old gnarled Maple tree in the front yard. Last summer she had painstakingly sanded, then refinished the original fence at the entrance to their property. The fence, made of hand hewn square logs was unique, and she wanted to preserve the original features.

In the back yard were two large imposing sheds that Moe called Quonsets. The white one, closest to the house, had been converted into a garage. The green one was Moe's. He always said that was his place to go, to putter and to relax. Lately he had been talking about building a small red barn, fencing off the back five acres, and buying each of the kids a pony. He was right as always. This was the perfect place to live and raise a family

The worst fight of their marriage had taken place several months ago, just before Christmas. She had gone to town to finish her shopping, and her bank card wouldn't work. Frustrated she had gone to the bank to get some cash, but their accounts were closed. Enraged she had driven home to confront him. Their once happy life now seemed to be one battle after another. She was tired of not knowing what to expect any more. The fact he was working on his motorcycle when she drove into the yard made her even angrier.

"Moe Browning, what the hell is going on around here? My bank card won't work. All of the bank accounts have been closed. What am I supposed to do for Christmas now?" she screamed at him in frustration.

"Relax baby girl, its cool."

"What do you mean it's cool? I stood there like an idiot trying my card and ended up walking out of the store leaving everything on the counter. Talk about feeling stupid. You had better explain yourself and fast."

"I closed the accounts in that bank. I didn't want them prying into my business. Some of those people working there are pretty nosey."

"So now what? I'm supposed to walk around like a pauper while you buy junk like this," she said, kicking the front wheel of the motorcycle.

"I said relax, I opened new ones on the other side of town at the Common Street Bank. If you need money, all you have to do is ask. I even set up an emergency fund for you in case you need money and I'm not here."

Reaching into his pocked he pulled out a wad of money, peeled of ten one hundred dollar bills and handed them to her. "There is more where that came from. If you need more, all you need to do is ask." he said proudly.

"Do you really think that I am going to come begging to you every time I need money? You are never here. How am I supposed to live like that?" she said bitterly. "You had better tell me what is going on? Where is this money coming from? Please Moe, just for once, tell me the truth."

"Get off my back Alicia. I am sick and tired of your nagging and prying. No matter what I do, nothing is good enough for you. I am working my butt off to keep you happy, and then you turn around and question everything I do. I have had enough of this crap" he said getting on his motorcycle. "I am out of here."

"Where do you think you're going?" She screamed at him moving to stand in front of his bike. "If you leave now don't even think about coming back."

"Get out of my way before I hurt you" he replied menacingly. She stepped to one side and he roared out of the yard.

Unknown to Alicia, a few miles down the road he pulled over to the side and stopped. Tears were flowing down his cheeks.

"Baby girl," he said to himself *"I've gotten myself into a real mess this time and I can't see a way out. I am doing my best to protect you and the children. That's why I can't tell you. The four of you are the most important things in my life. If I had listened to you and Tuk, none of this would have happened. Now I am in too deep. I hope you forgive me if you ever find out."* He wiped his eyes with the back of his hand, started his bike and roared off.

At four o'clock in the morning Alicia heard the motorcycle turn into the driveway then stop in front of their garage. She had been sitting in the dark waiting for him to come home.

Opening the front door, she watched him walk around the bike, and then turn toward the house. Running down the steps she threw her arms around him. Hugging her back, he whispered "I'm sorry" in her ear. Arm and arm they walked back into the house.

Moe sat down at the kitchen table, his head in his hands. Alicia reached over and placed her hands on top of his.

"Moe, tell me what is going on. Have you got yourself into some kind of mess with that Parker Johnson? Please, I need to know."

"Oh God, I am so sorry Alicia. I know I am hurting you and the kids. I didn't mean for any of this to happen."

Alicia stared at him for a long time. Then, pouring each of them a cup of freshly brewed coffee, she gently said "tell me. What's going on?"

"Stan, this guy who worked at the shop, I told you about him, remember? Well, one day he asked me to take a short side trip and deliver a package for him without Tuk finding out. Easiest three hundred dollars I have ever made. We needed the money - that's when Tuk was going through that bad spell. Sometimes, after he took off my payment, insurance and fuel there was barely enough for us to live on. I couldn't ask him for help because he was barely hanging on himself. This money was easy. I couldn't stand to see you worrying so much, and the kids going without all the time.

I made a dozen or so deliveries for Stan before he got fired. Through him I met another guy, and started making bigger deliveries. I would call him, tell him where I was going next, then meet him, and pick up the package if there was one."

"Didn't you ask what was in the packages?"

"I guessed, but I didn't want to know. I was making more money that I ever had in my life. I started hiding the amount because I didn't want you to see how much there was. That's why I changed banks. This is a small town, and I didn't want someone talking about where all of my money was suddenly coming from.

Then one day they asked me to go to Mexico – twenty thousand dollars for each trip I was willing to make. I wanted to quit then, but I was in too deep. They would give me an official looking bill of lading with Tuk's business name on it, and I would drive across the border. Then, in the middle of the night, I would bring back whatever they put into the van.

One of the guys, who worked as a border guard, was in on the deal, and he would pass me through without any fuss. I would drive to where they told me to go, someone would unload the van, and then I would continue on my way. Usually it only took a couple of hours.

"Didn't Tuk ask you why you were taking so long?"

"Yes, I usually told him I had to wait to get unloaded.

"Moe who are these people? You should go to the police, and tell them what you have been doing. Do you have any idea who you were working for?

"Baby girl, you don't need to know. I'm not exactly sure, but I think it is the Mexican drug cartel"

"Moe, do you really expect me to believe this story that you may be involved with a drug cartel. Who are these guys? You keep saying this guy, that guy, they must have names?"

"Alicia I love you and the kids more than anything in this world. If they find out I even told you this much you will be in danger. These are not nice men, and the less you know the better it is for all of us."

"Moe, I'm afraid. What if something happens to you? Please stop. Go to the police and tell them what you know. Think of me and the kids, because your secrets are tearing our marriage apart."

"I know Alicia. I really am sorry. I will find a way to get out of this mess, but in the meantime don't ask any more questions. Trust me."

They went to bed and, for the first time in weeks, made love. As Moe lay sleeping she laid awake thinking about everything he had told her. *"None of this makes any sense. Tonight I am relieved that Moe is home safely, but in the morning we will need to figure out what he should do."*

After that evening Moe refused to talk about what he was doing. Alicia tried to ask questions, but he ignored her. Then one evening he blew up. "Alicia, stop right now! Don't ask me anything more. I am sick and tired of your questions-tell me this, tell me that. This is none of your business. I don't want you to know any more than you do. I'm sorry I even told you that much. I will never forgive myself if something happens to you or one of the kids because they were trying to get back at me."

Alicia burst into tears at the sharp rebuke. Moe walked over to the door and put on his jacket. "Alicia, these are dangerous people" he said. "Believe me when I say I am doing my best to protect you and the kids. The best way I know how." Then he walked out the door,

Their life at home continued to disintegrate as Moe became more distant and more secretive. Once, while he was away, Alicia tried to get inside the green Quonset to see what he was hiding in there, but there was a padlock on the door. She tried to peek into the windows, but they were too high. Lately Moe was gone longer than usual; a trip that usually took two days was now taking three. She felt like she was walking a tight rope, afraid to say much when he was home and frantic with worry when he was gone.

Glancing at the clock, she realized it was time to get the kids up for school. Randy was the easiest to get up, but it usually took several calls to get Erin going. Sam was like the energizer bunny, happy, smiling and bouncing with energy.

"Is dad home yet?" asked Randy. "I want to show him the catapult I made in school."

"Maybe tomorrow Randy," Alicia replied uneasily. She didn't like deceiving them. "Erin, hurry up or you will be late."

While the kids ate their breakfast Alicia made their lunch, and gathered their coats and back packs. This hectic routine took place every morning.

"Erin, make sure Sam gets on the bus after school. I don't have to work today."

Three hugs, three kisses. A door slammed and it was quiet. Alicia watched them run down the driveway to the waiting school bus.

CHAPTER FOUR

Unconsciously Alicia tidied up the kitchen, made the kids beds and cleaned up the bathroom. This was her daily routine after the children left for school. She couldn't shake the sense of foreboding that had settled upon her. She knew that one phone call had changed their lives forever.

Standing in the shower, the enormity of what was taking place hit her. Even though she was standing with warm rain like water falling on her, she began to shiver uncontrollably. Still in a daze, she dressed in a pair of jeans and a shapeless white sweat shirt. Flipping her natural blonde hair into a pony tail, she grabbed her car keys off the cupboard and drove into town. She hoped going to Tuk's office would help her find out more about what was going on.

"Although Moe has explained, nothing is making any sense. If a border guard was in on this scheme how could he have been arrested? Maybe by the time I get to his office Tuk will be able to tell me this is all a big mistake, and we will have a good laugh. If this is a joke, it is a sick one."

Tuk had been the first person to give Moe a chance at a full time job after they were married. Moe didn't have any truck driving experience, but Tuk, one of the best drivers in the area, taught him everything he needed to know. Moe's dad had left when he was three, and Tuk became his substitute father. If it hadn't been for him, Alicia was sure Moe would have gotten into all kinds of trouble long before now.

Hesitantly she opened the door of the office. Tuk was standing at the coffee machine, his back to her.

"Tuk," she said tentatively.

He turned around with a start. He was unshaven, his eyes red as if he had been crying. His haggard face was a pasty whitish grey colour.

"Alicia what are you doing here?" he replied in a startled voice.

"I came to see if you have heard from Moe? I got a phone call this morning that doesn't make any sense. Please tell me this isn't true?"

"You bet your ass it's true. I am getting sick and tired of cleaning up that boy's messes. He's a grown man. He should be able to figure things out for himself. Last week he was out of radio contact for fourteen hours, and he was that much late on his delivery He almost cost me my contract with that firm. Not only that, his GPS was turned off. We had no idea where he was."

Alicia stood there as he continued his tirade. For the next few minutes he paced back and forth across his office muttering and swearing to himself.

She waited until he was finished then asked, "Tuk, what should I do?"

"How the hell do I know? Figure it out for yourself."

Alicia was stunned at his outburst. She turned to walk out of his office. This was not what she expected.

"Wait Alicia, I'm sorry. I am so frustrated right

now I can barely think. I don't know where his load is? I don't know if the police seized his truck or what? He has put me in a really bad situation, and I didn't mean to take this out on you. Sometimes I forget he is an employee and not one of my own kids. I wasn't thinking."

"I know" Alicia sighed as tears ran down her face. "I am sorry too."

"For now, why don't you just go home and wait for him to call, and when he does, we will go from there. Do you need any money? Moe has a pay cheque coming from last week and part of one for the end of this week. I can give you that."

"No, I'm fine right now. Please, let me know if you hear anything?"

"Sure thing," he replied curtly walking back into his office and slamming the door behind him.

Alicia was left standing there. *"He is really upset by all of this. I should have stopped and thought about that before coming here."*

She needed time to think. How could she get to Moe, and how could she help him? She drove to the water's edge of Coventry Lake, and paced back and forth along the shore line formulating and discarding ideas. She should hire a lawyer, but she didn't have enough money to pay for one. She knew she should go to the police, but if they asked her a bunch of questions, she wouldn't have any answers? Maybe she should get someone to watch the kids and drive down to the border, but she didn't know what crossing he was using. In the end, she decided she would have to talk to Moe first and find out what he wanted her to do.

As she was unlocking the front door the phone began ringing. She ran and managed to answer it on the fourth ring.

"Hi baby girl," she heard Moe say on the other end of the line.

"Moe is it really you?"

"Sure is. Look I need you to do something for me. I need you to call someone." Then he rattled off a phone number. "Tell them what has happened, where I am and tell them they better get me out of here. ASAP."

"Moe is this true? Are you really in jail? What were you thinking?"

"Alicia, get a pen and paper and write that phone number down. Ask to speak to Doug Lawson."

Alicia was crying, "Moe, I don't understand what is going on. Please tell me this is all a big mistake."

"Stop your damn crying. Can't you get it through your thick skull that I am in big trouble? I need you to make that phone call. Now!" He repeated the name and phone number. "Tell them to get their butts down here and bail me out. As soon as I can, I'll call you again."

Alicia was stunned by the cruelty in his voice. She repeated the number and name back to him.

"Now get on with it." He snapped back and then he was gone.

With trembling hands she dialled the number Moe had given her, noting it was long distance, and to an area code she was unfamiliar with.

"Lawson Petrie Law Firm" a woman's crisp voice

answered.

"I would like to speak to Doug Lawson please."

"May I inquire as to the nature of your call?"

"My husband, Moe Browning phoned and asked me to pass along a message to him."

"One moment please."

"Mrs. Browning, what can I do for you?" a male voice said on the other end of the line, "Doug Lawson here."

"My name is Alicia Browning. My husband is Moe Browning. He asked me to call, and tell you he has been arrested for smuggling drugs from Mexico. He is in jail, and needs someone to come and bail him out. Will you tell me what is going on here? I know this has to be a terrible mistake."

"I'll look after it, "he replied tersely and hung up.

Before Alicia had a chance to turn around the phone rang again.

"Moe?" she said picking up the receiver.

"No, it's me, Tuk. Have you heard from Moe yet?

"Yes, he called a few minutes ago. He asked me to phone a lawyer by the name of Doug Lawson to come and bail him out of jail. Tuk, do you have any idea what this is all about? If you do, please tell me. Who is this Doug Lawson? Where does Moe know him from?"

"Damn," he said. "Alicia, Moe has gotten himself mixed up with some bad people. Lawson is supposedly a lawyer for a moving company, but that's just a front. He really works for a gang in Mexico who are big into smuggling - drugs and people."

"You knew about this?"

"Not really. It's just that the pieces of the puzzle are starting to fall into place. My gut has been telling me Moe was into something, but until today, I had no idea what. This is bad news."

"Tuk, please tell me what I am supposed to do" she pleaded with him.

"Hang tight Alicia for a day or two until we see what happens. I'll see what I can find out on my end. Sooner or later someone will have to let me know where my truck and cargo are."

"I guess." Alicia replied quietly.

All afternoon Alicia thought about what she should say to her children. She didn't know what was going on, so how was she going to explain this to them? Should she wait and tell them later, or prepare them now? In the end, she decided the best thing to do was to be honest with them.

She waited until they had finished supper then said, "I have something I need to tell you. Your dad won't be home for a few more days. He was coming back from Mexico with his truck, and when they inspected his trailer at the border, they found some bad stuff in there. He has to stay there for a while until they figure out how that bad stuff got in there, and who put it there. Your dad told me he doesn't know what is going on. He is sure this is all a big mistake and will be coming home soon."

"What's a border?" asked Sam.

"A border is a line that separates two countries. In this case, Mexico is on one side of the line, we are on the other."

"What kind of bad stuff? Why does he have to stay there?" asked Erin.

"I don't know Erin. All I know is that he phoned, and said he was in jail, and that some of his friends are going to help him get out."

Randy sat there stony faced. Then he said, "You are lying. Dad wouldn't do something like that. He doesn't even go to Mexico."

"Randy, it's true; I am being honest with you and telling you all I know. I am having a hard time believing this too."

"You are wrong. My dad is not a bad man!" He jumped up from the table, stormed up the stairs to his room slamming the door behind him.

The girls left the table following him up the stairs. Alicia heard his door open and then it was quiet. She sat at the table staring at the blank wall for a long time

CHAPTER FIVE

For the next week life continued on as if nothing out of the ordinary was taking place. Alicia was kept busy working three days a week as a Teacher's Aide at the school. Parent Teacher week was coming up and each class was practising a presentation to put on for the school assembly they celebrated at the end of the week. There were costumes to help with, displays to put up, and decorating to be done in each class room. All of the children seemed unusually tense as they wondered what the teacher was going to tell their parents.

The days at home were hectic too - supper, homework, piano lessons, all the things that consume a busy family. The girls had stopped asking when their dad was coming home.

Each night Randy continued to ask, "Do you think he is coming tomorrow?"

Each night Alicia replied, "I don't know Randy."

The strain was beginning to show on Alicia. Her red eyes were rimmed with dark circles, her chin had broken out in blemishes, and there was a palpable sadness surrounding her. She shuffled when she walked, and her clothes were beginning to hang on her.

Even worse was the fact that people in town were finding out that Moe was in jail and why. Some of her friends began to avoid her. Other times they stopped talking when she entered the room, and she knew they were talking about her. It seemed that everybody had an opinion based upon the gossip, but none of her friends asked for the truth or how she was coping. Each, in their own way, were judging Moe based upon rumor and innuendo.

Early one Saturday morning Alicia's best friend, Sally Rogers, showed up at the house.

"What a surprise Sally. It's been ages since you were out here. Come in" Alicia said holding the back screen door open.

"I thought you could use a break, and so can I. My kids are driving me nuts. I thought if they had someone to play with, we might survive this weekend. I came to take all three Randy, Erin and Sam back to town with me."

"You don't need to do that."

"Oh yes I do. If not, I will be a raving idiot by supper time. This way they can keep each other busy and out of my hair. Besides, you look like you could use a little time to yourself."

Alicia felt guilty seeing Sally standing there. Since all of this commotion had started she had avoided her best friend as well as being seen in public. She went to town, did what was necessary, and returned home. The two of them had been close friends since high school, so there wasn't much they didn't know about each other.

After Sally left, Alicia tidied up the children's bedrooms, tossed a load of laundry into the washer, and then laid down for a nap. She was always tired these days. No matter how early she went to bed she didn't seem to have enough energy to make it through the day. To her, it seemed the only time she wasn't worrying was during the few brief hours she was able to sleep. Most nights she laid wide awake trying to figure out what she should do next. If the truth was known, she had no idea what she could do. She had to wait for Moe to come home.

After she awoke, she drove to town, and picked up a few groceries at the store and then drove over to Sally's house to pick up her kids.

"Thanks for taking the kids for a few hours Sally. We have been getting on each other's nerves the last few days. I really needed a break, and I appreciate you coming and taking them for the day."

"Thought so, I just made a fresh pot of coffee. Come in and stay for a while."

Soon they were sitting at the table in Sally's bright sunny kitchen, with steaming cups of coffee in hand, and a plate of freshly made chocolate chip cookies between them. The sunshine was streaming through the patio door, and Alicia could hear the happy shouts of the kids outside jumping on the trampoline.

"How are you doing Alicia?" Sally asked in a concerned way. "You look like you are carrying the weight of the world on your shoulders."

Alicia pondered the question for several seconds. Finally she opened up and told Sally the whole story. "Right now I am barely hanging on. I am at a complete loss about what to do. I haven't heard from Moe since the first time he called, and I have no idea where he is. I don't know what is going on, or why this is happening to us. I feel sick about the whole thing, that somehow this is my fault. I feel powerless. I have no control over what is happening to us, and each day I wonder what's coming next."

"Has Tuk heard from him? Bob keeps asking the boys at work, but if anyone knows anything they are keeping pretty quiet." Bob, Sally's husband was a mechanic who also worked for Tuk.

"Not a word. It's like he has disappeared off the face of the earth" Alicia replied fighting back tears. "Sally, I don't know what to do. I can't live on the money I am making at the school. Last week I used the last of my savings to pay the utility bills. Randy walks around glaring at me. Sam is whiny. Erin says nothing. I feel like grabbing them and yelling at them that this is not my fault. I'm not responsible for this problem, their dad is."

"They are just kids Alicia. They are hurting the same as you are, and you need to be patient with them. If you can't understand, how can they? Right now they need to know that you are not going any place, and that you are there for them. That means you have to pull yourself together."

"I know, but it's hard. You know Sally; I can't help thinking about what if I can't look after them by myself? What if welfare comes and takes them, and I never see them again?"

"You stop thinking that way right now. What is the old adage "what you think about you bring about," and you sure don't want that."

"Yes, I know, but what do I do if I lose everything? Moe will be furious with me. How am I going to find Moe? I need to find out what is true and what isn't? What if he never comes home again? What if.......?"

"Alicia, stop that right now. You have to be strong. Your kids need you to be. The best thing you can do is stop running from this, stop trying to understand, and face up to this new reality. Stop worrying about what could happen and handle the now, one day at a time. This will eventually end, but for now, you are going to have a bumpy ride. You will get through this. Remember that you are a survivor."

Alicia was still sniffling when they were interrupted by the opening of the back door. "Mom we are thirsty. We need a drink" Six hot dusty kids came trooping into the kitchen.

Sally insisted they stay for supper. She lit the fire pit in the back yard, and they roasted hot dogs and marshmallows. Dessert was orange pop floats. For the first time in weeks Alicia relaxed and enjoyed being with her children.

When it came time to leave, Alicia said "thanks Sally for the pep talk. This is the best day we have had for a long time. You always know how what to say that makes me feel better." Then she leaned over and gave her a big hug.

Sally put her hands on Alicia's shoulders, and looking right into her eyes said "you can get through this Alicia. Now that Moe isn't around, your kids need you more than ever."

Alicia was not sleeping well. When she did fall asleep she dreamed that she was ragged and filthy standing on a street corner begging for money, becoming more and more frantic as the day went on. Her cup was always empty. She didn't have any money to buy food for her family. At the end of each day, a man from Social Services always showed up demanding she give up her kids.

She would wake up in a cold sweat, her heart pounding in her chest. What if this came true? What could she do? How would she survive? If Moe didn't come home soon the bill collectors would start phoning. What would happen when she said to them "my husband is in jail, and you will have to wait until he comes home?"

Alicia knew she was letting her imagination run away on her. Automatically, whenever she was under stress, her mind would fixate on the worst case scenario, and then she allowed these thoughts to overwhelm her.

As the days passed she became more and more desperate. Where was Moe? Why hadn't he called again? Was he coming home at all? The not knowing was the basis of her fears and insecurity, but the longer he was away, the more anxious she became. Alicia knew that if she could get some answers she would know what to do from there. This way she was living in limbo.

 The small family quickly fell into a routine. On Saturday morning, if they had no urgent plans for the day, Alicia and the children wrapped themselves in blankets and watch cartoons. This gave them time to relax and spend time together. Sometimes they talked, but mostly they silently drew comfort from each other.

 One Saturday morning Alicia was startled out of her reverie by the ringing of the front door bell. She wasn't expecting anybody, and her first thought was that maybe, Moe had finally decided to come home,

"About time you got home Moe Browning," she said flinging open the door. But it wasn't Moe standing there. It was Cal Johnson and Billy Smith, two of the local police officers and with them was a man Alicia had never seen before.

He was a big man, with the shoulders of a football player, and stood at least six and a half feet tall. He had short blond hair, and was dressed in a black suit, white shirt and gray tie. His size alone made Alicia feel threatened. She understood immediately he was here in some sort of official capacity.

"Mrs. Browning? My name is Cliff Walker. I am a government agent working with drug enforcement. You are Alicia Browning, wife of Maurice Browning?"

"Yes."

"I have a warrant to search your property. We are following up evidence that stated drugs were being stored and transported from here. This warrant covers the sheds and Quonsets on this property. This whole procedure will go faster if we have your full cooperation. Do you have keys for the locks?"

"For all of them except the green one, Moe takes that with him. What makes you think there is anything here? I assure you there is not. Moe would never do that to us, he hates drugs."

"May I come in?" asked Mr. Walker. "I'll be here with Mrs. Browning until you are finished. Please be respectful of Mrs. Browning's property." he said to the other police officers.

Alicia started to relax. *"This Mr. Walker seems like a nice person, polite, gentle and considerate. Maybe he will give me some answers to the questions that are haunting me. Maybe he will be able to advise me on what to do from here."*

"Mrs. Browning, what can you tell me about Maurice's trips to Mexico? How frequent were they? Who did he meet? How long has he been going there? We will appreciate any information you can give us."

"Will my talking to you help Moe? Will it help clear this mess up so he can come home?"

"Yes ma'am. We will appreciate any information you can give us. If there has been a mistake, we want to correct it as soon as possible."

"First of all, I don't have any answers to your questions. I didn't know myself until the other day, when that phone call came, that he was going into Mexico. He is a long distance hauler so it's not unusual for him to be gone several days at a time. I have no idea who he was meeting. Usually someone called him on his cell phone, but I don't know who it was. He didn't allow any of us to touch his phone."

"You didn't find that unusual?"

"No. I thought it was his boss, or one of the other guys he worked with."

"He paid cash for this place. Where did he get the money?"

"I don't know. He had some money invested with Parker Johnson, and he told me that it paid off big. He never did tell me what they were, the Investments

I mean."

"Are you trying to tell me that he never talked to you about his plans or who he was meeting?"

"Yes."

"Let's go over this again Mrs. Browning. Try to think of anything he may have said or done. Have you seen any changes in Mr. Browning over the past little while?"

"Yes, he was becoming more distant and secretive."

"Why?

"I don't know. I thought he might have a girlfriend, and didn't want me to find out."

"Who did he talk to on his phone? Where did he go to meet them?'

"I told you, I don't know. I never heard any names, and when he was talking on his cell phone he usually went outside. I guess he didn't want me to hear his conversation or know who he was talking to."

"Did he tell you where his new found money was coming from?"

"No I already told you what I thought. If I asked any questions he would get angry with me, so after a while I stopped asking. I figured he would tell me when he was good and ready."

The sharp tone of his questions had put Alicia on her guard, and now she was being careful with her answers. Her earlier impressions of this man were false. He was becoming more insistent with his questions, and she was beginning to feel threatened. For two hours he sat there and asked her the same questions over and over. She didn't know any more than she had already told him.

"Mrs. Browning, I think you are lying through your teeth. I will find out the truth you know."

"Think what you want Mr. Walker. I don't know what you want me to say. I have told you repeatedly that I don't have the answers you are looking for."

"Mrs. Browning, I would like you to come to the police station and make an official statement. The boys are just about done out there. How does three o'clock this afternoon sound to you?"

"I'll come, but I won't be saying anything different. I honestly didn't know what Moe was doing. Please leave now."

After Cliff Walker and the police left Alicia phoned Sally and explained what was happening. "Sally, can I leave the kids with you while I make this dumb statement? I hope this will help clear Moe's name so that he will be able to come home soon."

Several hours later an exhausted Alicia picked up her children. At the police station they had taken her into a small office, handed her a pen and paper, asked her to write everything she knew about Moe's dealings, and then sign it. The only thing she could think about was the fact that he was hauling freight for Tuk.

While she was doing this Cliff Walker came in and repeated the same questions. She continued giving him the same answers. In the back of her mind she had a feeling that she wasn't helping Moe, in fact she was probably making things worse.

CHAPTER SIX

One week later, on a Sunday morning, Alicia was awakened from a deep sleep by the sounds of sirens and someone banging on her front door. Hastily she put on her housecoat and ran down the stairs. The children were awake huddling together in the hallway. Samantha was crying.

"Randy, take the girls into my room and close the door. Don't open it for anybody but me. Girls, you go with Randy and stay there."

"What's going on mom?"

"I don't know."

Through the living room curtains she could see the flashing blue and red lights of police cars. The banging on the door became louder and more insistent. She kept fumbling the lock on the door because her hands refused to cooperate. When she finally did get the door open Cliff Walker was standing there. Billy and Carl stood behind him, their hands on their guns. The yard was filled with vehicles, men dressed in suits and others in white coveralls.

Forcing his way into the house Cliff Walker towered over her shouting in his loud booming voice. "Alicia Browning, as an agent of the Government and under the Federal Recovery of Proceeds of Crime Act, I have a court order to seize your property, all contents within and surrounding. You and your children exactly have five minutes to vacate these premises." Now she understood how a small child must feel when looking up at an adult

Alicia looked at him stunned "What? I don't understand. I didn't give you permission to come into my house."

"It's easy lady. This is not your house any more, it's the governments. You have been lying to me all along so now you got five minutes to get your kids dressed and get out of here. You," he said motioning to Billy, "go with her and make sure she doesn't try to sneak a bunch of stuff out of here."

Suddenly Alicia was afraid for her own safety and that of her children. Her first thought was to get her children away from here. They didn't need to be part of this.

Running up the stairs she entered her bedroom and then knelt down in front of them. As calmly as she could she said. "Randy, Erin, Sam, I want you to go to your rooms and get dressed as quickly as you can. Wait for me in there until I come to get you."

"I want to watch TV," Sam whined, "my favourite program is on."

"No, you can't. Listen to me closely. Some men are here to look through daddy's things. The best thing you can do now is get dressed, and I will take you to Sally's until they are finished. How does that sound?"

"Not very good."

"Please don't argue with me, just do as I say. This is very important."

After shepherding the kids to their rooms, and moving as quickly as she could, she dressed in the first pair of jeans and t-shirt she saw hanging in the closet. Grabbing her leather jacket from the closet she put it on and then stuffed her wedding rings, diamond watch, bank books and loose change into her pocket. One at a time she went into the children's rooms making sure they were dressed and had jackets to wear. Taking Sam by the hand, all four of them walked bravely down the stairs, out the front door and got into her car.

She was beginning to feel calmer as she drove away when Sam started to cry. "I forgot my blankie." Can I go back and get it?"

"Sam you really don't need to take it with you. We will only be gone for a couple of hours."

"Please mommy?" Sam was crying in earnest. Alicia stopped and turned the car around in the middle of the road. She knew that every time Sam was upset or sick she clung to her blanket.

Her blanket was actually a faded pink and white baby quilt Mrs. Kelly had given her as a baby gift. The edges were ragged. The binding was coming off, even though Alicia had tried mending them numerous times. When she was younger, Sam would stand beside the washing machine and dryer patiently waiting until it was in her hands again.

Stopping in front of the house Alicia said to Sam "go get your blanket, and then come right out. It's in the family room."

Sam ran into the house, but was back a few minutes later empty handed.

"For goodness sake Sam, where is your blanket? We don't have time to fool around like this."

"That man wouldn't let me have it."

Alicia looked toward the door. Cliff Walker was

standing on the step, the blanket in his hand motioning at her to get going. *"What kind of man refuses to let a child have her security blanket?"*

"It's okay Sam. I will come back later and get it for you."

In her panic Alicia broke the speed limit driving into town. The only safe place she could think of to take the kids was Sally's. The children cowered in the back seat frightened out of their wits. As soon as the car stopped they were all out running up the sidewalk to Sally's front door. She pushed the doorbell, and then all of them rushed into the house. Sally and her children were sitting at the table eating breakfast.

Shocked Sally looked at Alicia. She had never seen her friend like this before. Fear and desperation were written all over her face.

"Sally, can I leave the kids here? I know they will be safe with you. I don't know when I will be back." The children looked bewildered and frightened.

"Alicia, what on earth is going on? Kids, all of you, go into the living room and turn on the TV," then turning to Alicia she said, "Girl, sit down before you fall down."

Alicia stumbled to the kitchen chair Sally offered her. She was shaking like a leaf. Sally poured a cup of coffee and placed the cup in front of her.

Alicia sat there silently, desperately trying to stop the panic rising in her throat. Then, after several minutes she said in a quivering voice. "They came and seized my house. Everything is gone. There is nothing left. Oh my God, what am I supposed to do now?"

"Slow down Alicia. Tell me what happened. Who took what? What is all gone?"

"Sally, they knocked on the door, got us out of bed. Said the government was seizing my home and property. It's all gone. We had five minutes to get dressed and out of there."

"Alicia you are not making any sense. Who is "they? Calm down and tell me."

With shaking hands Alicia lifted her coffee cup, spilling some on the table before she got it to her mouth. She took several large gulps. Even though the coffee was steaming hot she didn't seem to notice.

"That Cliff Walker, the drug enforcement guy I told you about. This morning he got us out of bed, and told me he had a court order that allowed him to take our home and acreage away from us. They had their hands on their guns and told us to get out. I couldn't think of any place to go except here. Sally, I don't know what to do."

"Did he give you an explanation of any kind?"

"He muttered something about the Drug Recovery Act. I don't know what he was talking about."

"Do you have any way of getting in touch with Moe? He needs to come home and deal with this."

"No. I don't know where he is. I haven't heard a word from him." Then looking at Sally she said sadly, "everything we worked for is gone. We are homeless and have only the clothes on our back. He wouldn't even let Sam have her blanket." Then she said, her voice rising hysterically, "can you imagine

59

a great big man refusing to give a child her blanket. What value is that? He stood there holding it in his hands as we drove out of the driveway like it was a prize trophy or something."

Refilling Alicia's cup Sally said, "You sit here for a few moments. Try to calm down. I 'm going to check on the kids."

Alicia could hear Sally talking to Randy in the living room. The longer she sat there the antsier she felt. She had to do something to stop them from destroying their lives, but what? *"I have to explain and make them understand that I didn't know what Moe was doing. He is going to be furious with me for letting this happen, but he should have come home and tended to this mess a long time ago instead of leaving it up to me."*

Alicia stood up when Sally came back into the kitchen. "I have to try and stop them," she said. "I'll explain as many times as I have to. Can I leave the kids here?"

"Alicia, stay here. Don't go back there. We'll find a lawyer who works on Sunday. In the meantime, I'll send Bob out to talk to that Cliff fellow. Maybe Bob can talk some sense into him."

Alicia paused, and then said." No! I have to go back. Sending Bob will only complicate matters. This is my fault. Moe is going to be really mad at me when he gets home."

"What makes you say that? Moe was the one who got caught."

"You don't understand. I didn't tell that Cliff Walker everything I know. Moe wanted out, he told me what he was doing and why he started. Stan knew. Maybe they should talk to him too. I have to go."

Sally moved and stood in front of Alicia. "Please stay here," she begged.

"I can't Sally. I have to try and stop this somehow."

Sally reached over, put her arms around Alicia and hugged her. "Leave the kids here. Take as long as you need to. Be careful my friend."

Alicia smiled weakly and was out the door. Sally stood at the window watching her drive away. Alicia and Moe had always been so happy, the perfect couple. What went wrong? More importantly, what was Alicia going to do now? She had seen Alicia upset before, but never as distraught as she was today.

When Alicia turned into her driveway yellow crime scene tape was strung across the road. She pulled over and parked her car on the shoulder of the road. Checking to see if anyone was about, she ducked under the tape and began running toward the house.

"Stop Alicia!" It was Amanda Eggers, a police woman on the local force. Her daughter was in the same kindergarten class as Sam. "Stop and stand still."

Alicia did as she was told.

"Amanda, this is a terrible mistake. Tell them this all wrong. I told that man time and time again I didn't know what Moe was doing."

"Alicia you need to understand something right

now. They have a court order that allows them to seize your house, everything in it, and everything on your property. You are trespassing on government land now. You can't be here, you have to leave."

"What's going to happen? What about us?" she said, her voice rising. "Why are they doing this? We don't even know if what they are saying about Moe is true. I can't stand by and let them take everything we have worked for. They have no right……..."

"I'm not sure. What I do know is that if Moe is found guilty, they will sell everything, cover their expenses and the rest will go into a fund to help the victims of crime. If he is innocent, all of your things will be returned to you."

"Damn it Amanda, I'm the victim here. My children are victims. How can they get away with crap like this? Tell me what I have to do to make this stop? What is going to happen to us? What do I tell my kids?" Then in a small voice Alicia begged, "Amanda please help me."

"Where are your kids now?"

"I took them to Sally Rogers. They are going to stay there until I get back."

"Go back to them. Once they have finished here I'll come and find you."

Alicia grabbed Amanda's arm. "Please believe me. I didn't know what Moe was doing. I can't believe this is really happening."

Taking Alicia's arm, Amanda led her back to her car. "Go back to your kids. They need you now. All of this is out of your control; there is nothing you can do. I will do what I can, but it probably won't be much."

Alicia went back to her car but didn't leave. She sat there all day watching as box after box was loaded into a moving van. She watched them smash in the door of the green Quonset. They took Moe's Harley motorcycle, filing cabinets, a second motorcycle and some guns. Alicia had never seen the second bike before, nor did she know that Moe kept guns in there.

Finally, at eight o'clock in the evening, she noticed Cliff Walker strutting toward her. She got out of her car and approached him.

"Why are you doing this to me? I trusted you. I told you everything I knew. I thought you believed me and were trying to help."

"Are you stupid or what? I have the authority to do this and I am, whether you agree or not. If you want to get any of this junk back you had better start telling me the truth. I am sick of your lies."

"I have told you everything I know. I don't know what else you want me to say."

"Then I guess you are out of luck. Go get those brats of yours. You have one hour to gather your clothes and personal effects. I'm warning you not to take anything else. Get moving. You are on the clock, starting now."

In a panic Alicia got into her car and drove blindly to Sally's to get her children. Amid tears, protests, and questions she took them back to the acreage. She knew Sally wanted to know what was happening, but she couldn't stop to explain things right now. She would explain later.

When she returned to her home the crime scene tape was gone. The police officer standing guard at the gate waved her through. The moving van was gone, as well as most of the police cars. She pulled up to the front door and she and the children got out. The yard seemed quiet and empty. Amanda was waiting for her at the door with a box of garbage bags in her hand. Alicia said nothing.

Turning to the children she said calmly, "Take these and put all of your clothes in them." She handed each of them a handful of green garbage bags. "Take your pillows, blankets and anything else you want and put them in here. Empty your drawers and closets. Be quick," she added, sending the children up the stairs to their rooms.

She ran up the stairs two at a time to her own room. Frantically she began dumping drawers on her bed, and adding clothes from the closet to the pile. She grabbed her photo albums and the wedding picture sitting on the dresser and stuffed them into one bag. Then going into the bathroom, she emptied the medicine cabinet, into the white wicker clothes hamper, and filled the rest of the space with towels and face cloths.

She could see her bedroom had been ransacked; her jewelry box and the crystal bedside lamps were gone. Her books had been dumped all over the floor. Even the mattress was askew.

Hurriedly she filled four garbage bags with her clothes, tied them closed, and placed them in the hallway outside her bedroom door. Then she went into Sam's room. It had been searched too. Sam was sitting in the middle of her bed clinging to her blanket and "Frizzy" her toy bear.

"Come Sam. Show me what you want to take." Once again, she emptied the closet and drawers stuffing everything into the garbage bags, and added those to the pile in the hallway. "Hang onto your blanket and bring Frizzy with you, we are going to see how Erin is doing."

Taking Sam's hand they went into Erin's room. Erin hadn't packed any clothes either. Her room was a mess and she was vainly attempting to pick her things up off the floor. Once again she dumped the contents of the closet and drawers on the bed and began stuffing more bags.

"Erin." she said, "Find your favourite toys and books and we will take them with us. Just pick a few because we can't take everything." The pile of bags in the hallway was growing larger.

Then she heard Randy hollering "Leave me alone. It's mine; my dad gave it to me."

Alicia entered Randy's room in time to see Cliff Walker snatch the Game Boy out of Randy's hand and throw him onto the bed.

Looking up, Randy said to her "Mom. Tell him dad gave that to me for Christmas."

"Shh Randy, it will be okay, I will get you another one."

Randy had put a few things in his bag. Alicia repeated her performance adding his bags to the growing pile in the hallway. Cliff Walker leaned against the door frame watching her.

Hugging Randy to her she looked at Cliff Walker

and stated, "You have gone too far. Don't you ever touch one of my kids again."

He looked at her, then at his watch and said, "Times up. Now get out."

It took each of them four trips up and down the stairs to move the garbage bags to the car. She still needed to get their coats and backpacks for school

On her final trip down the stairs she paused, looked around and felt sickened by the carnage that had taken place. The cushions and back of the sofa had been sliced open, their stuffing scattered all over the floor. Large holes had been punched in the walls and the curtains had been ripped down. The drawers of her antique china cabinet, left to her by Mrs. Clarke, were dumped all over the floor. Everything of value was gone; the television set, DVD player, the stereo system, Erin's piano. The two limited edition prints that hung on the wall behind the sofa were also gone.

In the family room, Randy's game systems were gone. The furniture in there had also been sliced open. The mahogany coffee table and end table were smashed into splinters. The large pink silk flower arrangement she had spent so much time making was trampled into the hardwood floor. She noticed that every ornament she had collected or been given was broken, the pieces scattered in all directions. Some of which she had been collecting since she was a young girl.

In a daze she walked into the kitchen. The stove and fridge were pulled away from the walls. The cupboard doors were all open, and the contents of the drawers were scattered all over the counter tops. There were broken dishes on the floor, and dirty footprints all over the white ceramic tile. Completely out of place were three large boxes filled to overflowing with food. She could see a container of milk and a box of cereal in one of the boxes.

"Take these with you to your car," said Billy, one of the local policemen.

She looked at him gratefully and asked, "did you do this?'

"No use seeing good food go to waste" he replied brusquely, picking up the heaviest of the boxes.

"Thank you" she said quietly.

He turned and walked toward the doo

Outside Cliff Walker and his cronies watched as she and the children dragged the garbage bags to the car. None of them lifted a hand to help the children as they struggled to drag the many bags out the door and across the lawn. Alicia opened the trunk and desperately tried to squash the boxes of food and all of the garbage bags into it. Those that wouldn't fit she stuffed inside the car, on the floor, the back window, and around the girls who were sitting in the back seat. The very last two she stuffed into the front with Randy. There was barely enough room for her to sit and drive.

She looked back at their home. There was nothing left there for them now. She laid her head against the steering wheel trying desperately not to cry.

CHAPTER SEVEN

Her hands were shaking so hard that she couldn't fit the key into the ignition of the car. On her third try the key finally slipped into the slot. Turning it, she put the car into gear preparing to drive away.

Looking into the back seat, and smiling reassuringly she asked, "Everyone buckled up? Everything is going to be fine kids; we will be out of here in a minute."

Suddenly Erin cried out "mommy look," and was pointing to the window.

At that same moment Cliff Walker began pounding on the driver's side window. Alicia could see he was very angry. After locking the doors she rolled the window part way down. "Now what?" she said sarcastically.

"Get out" he sputtered. "Get the hell out of that car."

"What? Why?"

"You heard me" he screamed at her, one hand on the window and the other on the gun peeking out from under his jacket. "Get your garbage, your brats and get out. The car stays here."

At first Alicia didn't move. She sat there in shock, unable to comprehend what he was saying to her.

He reached his arm in through the partially opened window, pulled up the lock button, and then yanked the car door open. Grabbing Alicia by the arm he pulled her out of the car where she landed in the dirt on her hands and knees. Frightened, the children scrambled out of their seats and knelt down around her.

"Mommy, mommy." Sam cried out, "Are you hurt?"

"No honey. I'm fine."

Pulling herself to her feet she brushed the dirt off of her pants. Angrily she stomped over to Cliff Walker, grabbed his arm and spun him around. "Don't ever touch me or one of my kids again or I will have your badge."

"Nice try lady. I can do whatever I want and there isn't a damn thing you can do about it. I could charge you with theft for trying to take that car out of here if I wanted to." He walked away, and then turning around, he looked at her he said "bitch," then continued walking away.

Humiliated, Alicia emptied the bags and boxes out of the car stacking them back on the lawn. To have this happen in front of people she knew ranked among one of the most embarrassing things to ever happen to her. Looking hopefully at the police officers standing around, she silently pleaded for help. Some watched impassively, others turned away when her eyes met theirs. The children stood on the lawn beside the growing piles of garbage bags. All three faces wore the same blank look of incomprehension. Her worst nightmare seemed to be coming true.

Cliff Walker walked back, glaring at her menacingly. "You tell me what I want to know" he snarled. "Tell me who your husband's drug connections are, and I will stop this right now."

Alicia looked up and replied quietly. "I don't

know. He didn't tell me. He said it was for my own protection. I have told you all of this before, why can't you believe me?"

Ignoring her, he tossed a set of keys to one of the policemen standing nearby. " Go hook up that red suburban to that old holiday trailer and bring it here." Then, looking at Alicia he said, "Don't say I never did anything for you. I checked the records and you have owned these two for more than five years. At least you will have a roof over your head. Take what you are given and get the hell out of here."

When the suburban and travel trailer were parked in the driveway two of the men standing nearby opened the door of the trailer and began throwing the bags and boxes inside.

Cliff Walker handed her the keys "two cars will escort you out. Don't you even think of setting foot on this property again? The government owns it now. If you do, I will have you arrested for trespassing and obstruction of justice."

Numbly Alicia motioned for the children to climb into the back seat of the suburban and then buckled them in. One car, its red and blue lights flashing, pulled in front of her and the other behind. As she was climbing into the driver's seat Cliff Walker called out "if you change your mind you know where you can find me."

When the three car procession reached the town limits the police cars left her. She pulled over to the side of the road, stopped, put her head on the steering wheel and cried. Deep sobs of rage and humiliation wracked her body.

From the back seat a little voice was pleading "don't cry mommy. Please don't cry."

CHAPTER EIGHT

"Mommy, I'm afraid" the little voice continued "Mommy please."

Alicia lifted her head from the steering wheel, then reached down and turned on the interior light. Turning to look at the children, she forced a weak smile and said "Mommy is okay now." Three pairs of huge dark brown eyes stared back at her.

In a small defeated voice she said "I don't know where to go tonight. I have to think about finding a safe place to park this trailer."

"I know," said Sam, "we can go to Waymart."

"Shut up Sam," said Randy "that's stupid. You think you can do everything at Waymart."

"You can too," retorted Sam "I seen trailers there before. Mommy, Randy called me stupid."

"Stop both of you. I need peace and quiet to think."

After a few moments of silence Alicia said, "You know what Sam, you are right. That is exactly where we are going to go. Tonight we need a place to sleep, tomorrow morning we will try to figure this out."

Sam turned to Randy and stuck her tongue out as if to say so there. Randy did the same to her.

Alicia started the suburban and resumed driving. Moe had always pulled the trailer and Alicia wasn't quite sure what to do. Then, as her confidence grew, she drove a little faster. The children, sensing her nervousness, were quiet in the back seat.

The Waymart, built four months ago, sat at the

bottom of a large hill. The narrow road down to the parking lot was shaped in an S curve with a sharp turn at the top and another at the bottom. Alicia remembered Moe always telling her to "turn wide."

The first turn was the hardest. She inched down the hill at five miles per hour until she was safely at the bottom. Only then did she realize she was holding her breath. The parking lot was empty. She manoeuvred the suburban toward a back corner, and then made a wide circle so the trailer door faced the dimly lit parking lot.

When she finally came to a stop she remarked "thank goodness I cleaned and stocked the trailer this spring. The only item missing for tonight is water, but if I remember correctly, I put a case of bottles under the sink for drinking."

It was dark and late when the four of them tumbled out of the suburban. They were all mentally, physically, and emotionally spent. She decided to leave the trailer hooked to the suburban because that would be easier than trying to hook everything back up in the morning. Besides, she wasn't quite sure what to do. That was one more thing Moe always did.

Cautiously she opened the door to the trailer, reaching for the light switch on the side wall. A bright light flooded the small space. The garbage bags and boxes, which the police men had so carelessly tossed in, were scattered from one end to the other.

Motioning the children to follow her, she cleared a path by piling bags on top of each other. The boxes went on top of the small counter top.

Looking around she realized this was going to be their home for now. After eleven years, this was all that was left – a beat up old suburban that used oil, and a ten year old twenty-nine foot long travel trailer.

Despite its age, the trailer was in good shape. At one end was a bedroom with a queen size bed, two small closets mounted to the wall on either side of the bed, and a shelf for a small television set. A row of cupboards, centred between the closets, hung over the head of the bed.

At the other end was a three piece bathroom with a tub so small an adult could barely fit in it. Thankfully there was a shower nozzle also. Two bunk beds and another small closet were located on one side. The top bunk was a single bed, the bottom a double. Folding doors separated the bedrooms from the living area and provided a small amount of privacy.

The only door into the trailer opened into the kitchen. Along the left side was a fridge with a separate freezer on top. Opposite the fridge was three burner propane stove with a microwave in the cupboard above. On the wall by the sink, the top and bottom cupboards allowed for a small counter surface to work on.

Beside the stove was a sofa with another bank of cupboards located above it. The sofa area slid out which added another two feet of floor space. Beside the fridge was an eating nook with two bench seats and a table. A small entertainment center containing a television set and a DVD player was above the table. The bench seats lifted for more storage, and if necessary the table could be made into another bed.

"Mommy, I'm hungry" said Sam. Erin and Randy were unusually quiet. All three were sitting at the table looking at her.

"I know sweetie. Let me take a look and see what I can find."

She dug through the boxes until she found the box of cereal and the container of milk she had spotted earlier. Reaching into the cupboard above her head she took out three red plastic bowls. Filling them with milk and cereal, she placed one in front of each child. Although she hadn't eaten since the previous evening, the thought of food made her feel nauseous. From under the sink she pulled out four bottles of water, using two to make a pot of coffee.

Turning around, she saw Sam had fallen asleep, her head resting beside the partially eaten bowl of cereal. Erin was yawning.

"Erin, please go and pull back the covers on the bottom bunk so I can put Sam to bed."

She picked Sam up and gently laid her in the bed, removing only her shoes. Erin, also fully clothed, crawled in beside her sleeping sister. Alicia kissed her on the forehead and tucked the covers around them. Erin was already asleep. Reaching up she pulled back the covers of the top bunk and plumped the pillow.

"Your turn now Randy" she said.

"I'm not going to bed. I'm going to stay up all night and make sure that man doesn't come here."

"Honey, he won't," Alicia assured him, her eyes filling with tears. "He doesn't even know where we are."

Randy sat there yawning, his eyes glued to the door. Finally he got up, checked to make sure the door was locked and all of the blinds were closed.

"Now he can't see us," he said climbing into his bed. "Mom, if he comes you call me."

Alicia felt like her heart was breaking into two pieces. This was all wrong. In a frantic burst of activity she began putting the boxes of food away into the cupboards and refrigerator. She also rearranged the garbage bags, piling them on the sofa.

Then, her energy flagging, she poured a cup of coffee and sat down with her elbows on the table, both hands cupped across her mouth staring at a spot on the opposite wall. She was passed crying. There were no tears left.

As she sat there she could feel the panic beginning to rise in her chest. She gasped for air; her heart pounding wildly.. She felt light headed, and in the back of her mind thought she must be having a heart attack. Pushing herself away from the table she unlocked the door and ran outside. She felt like she would suffocate if she stayed inside the trailer for another minute.

Standing in the parking lot she gulped the cool night air. Finally her panic began to recede, and she felt herself beginning to calm down.

Filled with nervous energy she paced back and forth. Random thoughts kept popping into her head. *"Where is Moe. He has no home to come to. We are living in this trailer and are basically homeless. How am I going to look after these three kids? Why did I let Moe make all of the decisions? I should have stood up to him more. If I had, maybe I could have prevented this. What am I going to do now?"*

She was back where she had been at six years of age -

alone, frightened and powerless. The perfect world she tried so hard to create was shattered like a glass ball, the fragments lying at her feet. All of the insecurities she had known as a child came rushing back into her body.

Looking upward she said "Oh Lord, help me. I don't even know how to start."

CHAPTER NINE

Sometime during the night Alicia came back into the trailer, laid down on the top of her bed, covered herself with her leather jacket and fell asleep. The children's voices woke her up in the morning. Every bone in her body ached, especially her left arm, the one Cliff Walker yanked on to pull her out of the car. Both knees were skinned from landing on the ground. Her head felt like someone was using a jack hammer inside her skull.

"I want to go home I don't like it here," she heard Sam say.

"Me either," replied Erin

"You can't," said Randy.

"Why not, Randy?" asked Sam.

"Because we don't have a home any more, those men took it away from us."

"I don't want to live here. I miss my bed."

"Have to from now on."

"Randy," asked Erin, "do you think daddy is really a bad man? That policeman said he was."

"I don't," interjected Sam.

"Me either," replied Randy "he is with bad people just like mom said. It's all their fault."

"Mom was crying last night. I woke up and heard her. Do you think she will always be sad now?" asked Erin.

"For a long time I think, but not forever, just until daddy comes home. I will be sad too until he comes back."

"Me too." said Erin

"Me three" said Sam, and then she giggled. More seriously she asked. "Do you think daddy can find us here? He doesn't know where we are."

"Yes, because he will keep looking until he does. Mr. Tuk will tell him where we are."

Listening to her children talk this way tore at Alicia's heart. They were so young and innocent. There was no valid reason they had to be uprooted and removed from everything they knew and loved.

A wave of deja-vue swept through her. She was six years old when her mother disappeared, and she was walking up the front sidewalk to her first foster home. She knew how they were feeling, but she had no answers for them.

She got out of bed and gingerly walked into the kitchen. From under the cupboard she got four more bottles of water. She poured two into the kettle to heat so they could wash their hands and faces, the other two she used for another pot of coffee.

"No school today kids." she announced "We have some errands to run, and I want you with me. Randy, you and Erin figure out which bags are yours and put on some clean clothes. When you are finished put your bags on top of your bed until we figure out what to do with them. Come Sam, let's see what we can find for you."

Eventually the children were changed, and Alicia washed their hands and face with the warm water from the kettle. She divided the last of the cereal and milk between them.

While they were eating, she washed as best she could, and then changed her clothes putting on the first clean ones she found. She shuddered looking at the freshly opened and dumped bags, but left them where they were. She felt overwhelmed by too much stuff in too little space.

Last night she had decided that the first thing she was going to do this morning was go to the bank and withdraw the money Moe had put in the emergency fund for her. She and Randy went outside, and with a great deal of perseverance, got the suburban unhooked from the trailer.

She drove straight to the Common Street Bank and waited outside until it opened. Feeling extremely anxious, she knew that any future decisions, and the welfare of her children depended upon how much money Moe had put away. Once inside, she sat the children in the red plastic chairs lined up along the side wall. Admonishing them to sit quietly until she was finished, she walked up to the teller.

"My name is Alicia Browning. My husband Maurice Browning opened an account here for me some time ago. I want to take some money out of that account."

The teller typed her name into the computer. "Excuse me Mrs. Browning. I have to get the manager for an override. I'll just be a minute."

Alicia watched her walk in the manager's office, say something to him, and then they both came out.

"Mrs. Browning," said the manager. "Please come into my office."

He opened a gate and ushered her in. After they were both seated he said "Mrs. Browning, I understand you wish to withdraw a sum of money from your account."

"Yes."

"We do have an account with a balance of fifty thousand dollars with your name on it. The problem is that I can't give you any of the money because the government; has put a hold on it."

"A hold put on by the government? I don't understand. Are you telling me that I can't have any own money?"

"Yes. If your name was the only one on the account I could give it all to you, but your husband's name is there also. The government has frozen every account in our bank with his name on it."

"Is there anything you can do to get this hold taken

off? I need to find a place for me and my kids to live."

"I am truly sorry Mrs. Browning but there is nothing I can do to help you. I wish I could, but my hands are tied."

Without saying a word Alicia stood up, shook his hand, turned and walked out of the his office and out of the bank The children got off their chairs and followed her.

The bank manager followed her out of his office and watched her leave. There was nothing he could do, but he wished there was. He felt helpless because she appeared so desperate. There was no way he could go against the government order. He would lose his job if he did.

"Oh my God" she cried out loud. "I wonder if they did the same to my accounts at the Mid-town Credit Union?" Feelings of desperation, rage and anxiety were rippling through her body.

Urging the children into the car she drove through town at breakneck speed. Not even thinking, she parked the car in a handicap zone, which was something she would never do under normal circumstances.

"You kids stay here" she said as she got out and ran to the bank. Pausing at the door, she took a deep breath, walked inside, and approached the teller.

"Hi Alicia," Shelley Brown, the teller, said to her "How are things going today? What can I do for you?"

"I would like a balance on my accounts please." Inside she was pleading "*please be there, please be there*"

"You have thirty dollars in your chequing account and five hundred and ten in your savings."

"I would like to withdraw five hundred please."

Shelley counted out the five hundred in fifty and twenty dollar bills and handed them to her. "Have a nice day," she said. "Next."

Alicia grabbed the money and went back to her suburban. At least they hadn't got around to taking that yet. From the bank she drove out to Tuk's trucking business,

"Kids you wait for me while I go into to see Mr. Tucker. I won't be long. I am going to get your dad's pay cheque, and no fighting while I am gone either."

"I want to come too," said Sam, "Randy is mean to me."

"Am not," replied Randy.

"Please stop. This is not easy for any of us. Randy, and stop teasing your sisters."

Alicia got out of the suburban and walked hesitantly into the office. This was her last resort. She wasn't sure how much money Moe had coming, but she also didn't know how she was going to live on the few dollars she had withdrawn from her own account.

Tuk was on the phone so she waited outside of his office until he finished his call.

"Tuk," she said, "can we talk?"

"Yeah, come on in, "he replied gruffly.

Taking a deep breath she said, "The last time I was here you offered me Moe's pay cheque, can I have it today? There is a problem at the bank that needs to be cleared up. Until he comes home I can't take any money out."

"Can't help you Alicia" he said curtly.

"But you offered."

"Well things are different today."

"But...."

"Alicia, all I can tell you is that Moe's stupidity has put my business in jeopardy. I have worked too hard getting this business set up, and I am not going to let some greedy idiot pull me down with him. There is nothing I can do for you. Government agents were waiting for me when I got here this morning. They took all of my records concerning Moe, including the last full pay I owed him. I have nothing for you."

"Tuk, I am so sorry Moe has done this to you."

"There is nothing for you to be sorry about. He committed the crime, and we are all going to have to pay for his stupidity. Close the door on your way out."

Alicia looked at him for a minute, then turned and walked out, quietly closing the door of his office behind her.

"Oh Lord. What am I going to now? He was my last hope" she muttered to herself.

When she got back to the suburban Randy asked "Did you get dad's cheque mom?"

"No I didn't" she answered putting the suburban in gear.

What Alicia couldn't see was Tuk angrily pacing back and forth in his office. He could see how desperate she was, but that Cliff Walker fellow had threatened to close him down if he helped her. In the end, he made the choice of not helping Alicia in hopes that his business would be safe. This was one hell of a thing for Moe to do to his wife, his kids and to him. They were like family to him, and he had just turned her out of his office.

"I hope one day she will forgive me" he muttered to himself.

Next Alicia drove out to the highway where the R V parks were located. Her plan was to find an inexpensive spot and move the trailer there. She was completely discouraged by the signs that read "Full Hook Up $30 per night". The five hundred dollars in her purse wouldn't last long at those rates.

"Mommy, I'm hungry" complained Randy "Can we got to Macdonald's?

Alicia glanced at her watch and realized it was well passed lunch time. She went through the drive through ordering burgers, fries and a pop for the children and a cup of coffee for herself.

"Hey guys, since we are so close to the lake how about if we go have a picnic."

She parked in the Public parking area, and they walked toward the beach until they found a table. After lunch the children played on the playground equipment. Questions without answers were racing through her head *"If I stay in the parking lot how long will it be before they ask me to leave? How am I going to give the children a normal life this way? Who can I go to for help?"*

At one point she started to giggle over the absurdity of her situation. She had felt like Cinderella when she married Moe, now her prince charming had left taking both glass slippers with him.

"First things first" Alicia said to herself as she drove back to the Waymart parking lot.

She and Randy managed to hook the trailer back up to the suburban, and then she drove to the service station across the street. There she filled the trailer's holding tank with water and purchased some bread and sandwich meat for the kid's lunches. She had already decided they would be better off going back to school in the morning. They all needed to get into a regular routine as soon as possible. She still had one more day before she was scheduled to go back to work. When she was finished she drove back to the parking lot, and manoeuvred the trailer into a different spot, one that made her presence less noticeable.

The high embankment, which encircled the back side of the parking lot, blocked the noise of the traffic from the nearby streets. On the front side she parked between two areas containing young trees and flower beds filled with white and pink flowers. She realized this was actually a very pretty place for travellers to stop. The trailer door now faced the embankment, thus giving them a little bit of privacy. She hoped that by parking in this new spot their presence would go unnoticed for a long time.

Back at the trailer the kids climbed the hill around the parking lot while she struggled to find a place to put their clothes and toys. No matter how hard she tried there was too much stuff for the small space.

They went to bed early. Alicia was exhausted to the point of barely being able to keep moving. Even then, sleep eluded her for a long time.

The next morning she drove the kids to school promising to be there to pick them up afterwards. She spent the morning sorting through the many garbage bags taking out only what was necessary for their basic needs. What wasn't needed, she put into the storage compartments at the front and rear of the trailer. Then she walked to the store and purchased one large and one small plastic container for each child. Their clothes would go into the large container; the small one would give them a place to put their personal items.

Slowly, over time, a semblance of order began to emerge. During the day, the containers would be out of sight on the beds. At night they would stack them on top of the table benches. The current sleeping arrangements would do for now. The trailer was already looking better and more organized which made her feel better. This was a confined space for four people, but she assured herself they would be able to manage for a short period of time.

When finished, she took a quick shower then walked back to the store to get milk and other food items she needed. As she was pushing the cart back to the trailer she saw a police car pull up. It was Amanda.

"What do you want?" she commented bitterly. "Are you here to rub in what went on, and how I am forced to live here?"

"I know I deserved that Alicia, but I was only doing

my job."

"I know. Sorry."

"First, the official reason I am here. A week from today you are requested to show up at the Drug Enforcement office for an interview. At that time they will fully explain what they are doing, and why. You will also be given an opportunity to claim what is yours, and what is necessary for the well-being of your children. Here is the address and time. It is also my duty to inform you that you should take a lawyer with you."

"Fat chance of that. Do you know any lawyer willing to work for free? I have no money Amanda. Every bank account with Moe's name is frozen. There is even a hold on my kid's accounts so I can't touch them. For now we have to live on what I make at the school, which isn't much."

"Alicia I am so sorry. Is there anything I can do to help you? That Cliff Walker guy is being totally unreasonable. He is trying to push his weight around our department too, which is not going over very well. It's disgraceful the way he is targeting you. Alicia, you need to find a way to fight him, or you will be left with nothing."

Later that evening Amanda came back with her husband Joe. He showed her how to level the trailer, and donated a long yellow long extension cord to plug the trailer into the courtesy electrical plug nearby so that they now had power. Then he set up the antennae, and got the television set and DVD player working for the children. He showed her how to empty the sewer, how to control the air conditioning, and how to check the propane tanks. She was grateful for their help.

"Amanda I can't thank you enough for you and Joe coming here, and for all you have done."

"Keep this to yourself. I'm not sure if this is standard

police policy, and I certainly don't want to give that Walker guy any more ammunition. Alicia, you are going to have to stand up to him or he is going to make your life a living hell until he gets what he wants."

"Hey girls, enough of that serious talk," Joe said. Then to Alicia he added "you should be good for a few days. Phone the guy on this business card. He is a friend of mine who services the RV parks with water and sewer services. Call him and see what kind of a price you can get. I'll put in a good word for you. Are you ready to go Amanda?"

Slowly over the next few days their life settled into a routine, but Alicia felt like a heavy dark cloud had descended on her shoulders. She went to the school every day because she had to, this was her only income. She felt as though she was barely functioning. Everything she did seemed to take too much effort. She would forget what she was doing, where she was going, or when she arrived at one place, she forgot why she was there. She knew she was going through the motions, barely making it from one day until the next, scarcely able to do what needed to be done. Most of the time, completing even the simplest of tasks was difficult.

Every day she phoned the number Moe had given her and left the same message.

"This is Alicia Browning. If you know where my husband Moe is I need to talk with him. He can call me on my cell which will be on twenty four hours a day," She hoped that Moe would call soon to tell her he was on his way home.

CHAPTER TEN

"Alicia, Steve wants to see you in his office before you leave." June Adams called out to her as she was leaving the school staff room. It was Friday, pay day, and the end of a long week. She had promised to take the kids to a movie this evening. It had been a long time since they had done anything special together.

Steve Wilson, the school principal, was one of the nicest people Alicia had come to know. She had worked at the school for three years, and found it rewarding to work with children. She knew Steve was pleased with her work because he had told her so on many occasions.

"Hi Steve, what's up?" she said bouncing into his office. "I'm sure glad it's Friday. This has been one long busy week."

Seeing the distressed look on his face she stopped talking. "Is something wrong? Has something happened?"

"Sit down" he said quietly. His face was flushed, and he stared down at his desk as he spoke. "Alicia, the superintendent of the school faxed me a letter today. I have been instructed to inform you that your services are no longer wanted here. I am to personally escort you off the school property and you are not to return unless specifically requested to do so by one of your children's teachers. Your personal effects and supplies will be boxed up over the weekend and will be delivered to you,"

Alicia was in shock. "Why? Have I done something wrong? Steve?"

"You haven't done anything wrong Alicia. In fact, your work is exemplary. A Mr. Walker met with the school board and convinced them that they couldn't take a chance of having a drug dealer's wife working in the school. The welfare of the children must come first." Then he added "Alicia. I hate having to be the one to deliver this news, but I have no choice. Can you understand that?"

"I only understand one thing." she replied angrily, "I have been tried, found guilty and am being punished for something I had no part of. You know how much I love these kids. I would never do anything to hurt them. Please Steve, talk to them again. Explain to them I need this job to support my own family. Tell them I didn't know what Moe was doing."

"I am sorry Alicia. I can't"

"You can't, or you won't?"

"I can't. I have to do what they tell me. I tried to talk them out of doing this, but I was told to mind my own business. If I didn't my job was on the line."

Alicia rose from her chair looked at Steve, and said defiantly. "I can escort myself out thank you." Then she turned and walked out of the office. For some reason her life was unravelling and she didn't know why.

Once back in her suburban she screamed, pounding the steering wheel with her hand. *"I didn't do anything. I didn't do anything. What am I going to do now? What am I going to tell the kids? Oh God where do I go from here?"*

Suddenly she looked up and saw her children standing by the suburban, waiting to get in. Her promise to take them to the movie was forgotten. All she wanted to do was crawl into bed, pull the covers over her head, and make the world go away.

She drove straight to the trailer without saying a word. The kids, not knowing why she was upset seemed to argue more than usual in the back seat. Alicia was angry beyond words. The last thing she wanted to do was take her frustration out on the kids so she ignored them. Things were going from bad to worse. What else could go wrong she wondered?

Once in the trailer she called the kids over to her. "Something happened at school today that I want to tell you about. Mommy won't be working there anymore. Steve, Mr. Wilson says that right now I can't work there."

"Is it because of daddy?" asked Erin.

"Yes sweetie. When he comes home, we will get everything straightened out."

"I hate daddy," said Randy.

"Oh Randy don't say that."

"Why not, if he loved us he would have come home already. He doesn't have any right to do what he is doing. When he comes home, I'm going to tell him how much I hate him."

Erin came over and began patting Alicia on the shoulder. "It's okay mommy. You will find a new job."

Alicia smiled weakly. Children always seemed to

put a different perspective on a situation.

Early the next morning her cell phone rang,

"Hi baby girl, how's it going?"

"Moe is that you? Where are you? When are you coming home?"

"Yeah it's me. I need you to tell me what is going on there. Have the police come around yet?"

"Moe, everything we worked for is gone. The government came and took it away."

"What do you mean everything?"

"A guy from Drug Enforcement came to the house, kicked us out and confiscated everything we had. They let me keep the old suburban and travel trailer, and that is what the kids and I are living in. We are living in a Waymart parking lot if you can believe that."

There was silence on the other end of the line.

"Moe, I got fired yesterday. That same guy went to the school board, told them I was selling drugs for you in the school, and they fired me."

"I left you some money for emergencies, did you get that?"

"No. The bank said the account was frozen and I couldn't have any."   She was disturbed to hear him laughing and talking to someone in the background.

"Sorry baby. What were you saying- that you can't get any money from the bank? I'll look into that."

"Moe where are you?

"In Mexico, got me a little place just across the border."

"México, what the hell are you doing there?

When are you coming back to straighten out this mess you created?"

"That's what I phoned to tell you. I'm not. Life is good here. Why would I want to trade it away?"

"Stop teasing me. I need you to come home and help us; we can't go on living this way. If this is a mistake you need to straighten everything out."

Suddenly his voice turned harsh "I told you, I'm not coming back. To what, a bunch of snot nosed kids, and beating up and down the road twenty fours a day making peanuts. I won't even get started on how you hold me back. This is my kind of life, and I am enjoying every minute of it."

"How dare you speak to me like that? Who the hell do you think you are? You walk out on us; leave us in this mess and now what? Don't think you can come crawling back like a worm, when the good times are over and you have no place to go. I won't have you. Moe, how did you get us into this?"

"For God's sake Alicia, stop your damn nagging. That's all you ever do. Moe this, Moe that! I need a life, and it sure as hell isn't there with you."

Trying a different tactic Alicia begged "Moe, please come back. We can work this out. You can explain it was all a misunderstanding, that you didn't know what was in your van. I thought you had stopped making those special deliveries. You promised me you would."

"Are you that stupid Alicia? Where did you think the money kept coming from? I have been doing this for years, only this time I screwed up. I was running two log books and handed the guy at the border the wrong one. They had me for driving more hours that I was allowed. That's why they searched the truck. Good thing too. For the first time in my life, I am happy and having a good time. Couldn't do that with you hanging around all the time."

"Moe, please come home. I need you, the kids need you. Doesn't that count for anything?"

"Gotta go." he said, and abruptly hung up. Quickly she checked her cell phone to see if there was a number, but all that showed up was no ID.

Moe hung up his phone. Wiping away the tears stinging his eyes he thought, "Alicia, if only you knew how much I love you and our kids. I would give anything to be back home with you right now."

Then, shrugging his shoulders, he remembered his reasons for slipping back into Mexico. This way his family was safe. As long as he was there, nobody would bother them. When an opportune moment came along he would go home where he belonged. He had no choice but to talk to her that way. There was always somebody in the room who could be listening.

From that moment Alicia felt a darkness descend upon her. He had been lying to her all this time. What a fool she had been. She felt her world was disappearing, that she had no reason to keep on living.

Like a robot she got the kids up, and drove them to school. At the end of the day she picked them up. Most days she had trouble forcing herself to do anything. Her feelings alternated between anger and pity. She screamed at the walls, calling Moe every name she could think of, and then cried for hours because she was sorry. Her pain made her life a living hell. She felt as if she was caught in a terrible nightmare and couldn't wake up.

Slowly, over the next few days, her sanity returned. She forced herself to accept the fact that Moe wasn't coming back soon.

On the following Monday morning she dropped the kids off at school, and then, gathering her courage, walked to the Waymart store and applied for a job. She could barely afford to work for six dollars an hour, but it was better than nothing. She still needed money for food, and to pay for the for the water delivery and sewer pump out every week.

Two days later she was called in to work unloading freight for five hours a day, three days a week. She was still able to pick up and drop off her kids at school every day.

Once again, a bit of normalcy returned to their lives. Each of them welcomed the routine. Alicia was surprised, she actually liked her job. The work wasn't hard but was steady, and the time passed quickly.

Once she had seen Cliff Walker come out of the men's bathroom, another time out of the manager's office. Each time she turned and walked the other way making sure he didn't see her.

Randy was getting harder to handle. He was belligerent and talked back most of the time. She could see that he was a very angry young man. Samantha was whiny, clinging to Alicia for assurance. Erin simply ignored her.

One day, after school, Erin began to cry as soon as she climbed into the back seat of the suburban. Alicia let her be until they got home. Once back at the trailer Erin threw herself on her bed and buried her head in the pillow.

"Erin, what's wrong?" Alicia asked, sitting on the edge of the bed beside her.

"Leave me alone."

'Please talk to me Erin. I can't help you if I don't know what's wrong."

"The kids at school are calling me a druggie. They said you and daddy are selling drugs, and that's why you got kicked out of the school."

"Erin, that's not true. I told you exactly what happened."

Sitting up and looking at her mother Erin asked, "Then why did we lose our house? Why do we have to live in this dumb trailer in a parking lot? They said you and daddy are going to jail. What will happen to us then?"

"Nobody is going to jail. As soon as your dad comes home he will fix everything and they will stop talking."

Randy and Sam both came into the bedroom. Sam sat on the bunk bed beside Erin looking sad. Randy was leaning against the wall with an angry scowl on his face

"This is your fault," Randy said to Alicia.

"Why would you say that? That's not what this is about."

"I heard that man say that if you tell him what he wants to know we can go back to our house. I also heard dad say one time that if you didn't ask for so much, he wouldn't have to work so hard."

Alicia said nothing. The kids needed someone to vent their anger on. They had been keeping their feelings bottled up for a long time. *"Finally they were expressing how they feel. I knew this had to happen one day, but Randy's words cut like a knife. Maybe I didn't explain well enough. How can I expect them to understand when I can't? Am I passing on my fears and insecurities to them?* She understood why he was so angry. First their dad had left, and emotionally she had left them too

CHAPTER ELEVEN

The next morning Alicia made a point of being extra cheerful. She teased the kids, and spent extra time braiding Sam's hair, and telling Randy how proud she was of him. She dropped them off at school a little later than usual then had to hurry so she wouldn't be late for work. Things were starting to look up. Maybe they would come out of this; certainly they were all in a better mood today.

After school she waited for her children to come out. When they hadn't show up thirty minutes after school was dismissed she began to feel anxious and confused. *"Where were they?"*

Even though she wasn't permitted in the school, she got out of her suburban, entered the building and walked directly to Steve's office. She didn't care what they tried to do to her; she was going to find out where her kids were. She knocked on the office door, and then walked in. Old habits were hard to break.

"Steve, do you know where my kids are? Did they have to stay late or what?"

A funny look crossed his face, and he began to shake. "Alicia, you are not supposed to be in here."

"I know, but never mind that. School has been out for a long time and my kids haven't come out yet."

There was silence, and then Steve, looking at the floor, said "they aren't here."

"What do you mean not here? I dropped them off myself this morning. I watched them walk through the doors."

Taking a deep breath he said "A fellow by the name of Cliff Walker and a lady from Social Services were waiting in my office with an apprehension order. As soon as your children entered the building they took them away. There was nothing I could do to stop them."

Alicia felt a sharp pain in her stomach like someone had driven a knife into her. She staggered to a chair and sat down staring at him.

"Alicia you have to leave," Steve said. "I'm supposed to call the police if you come onto school property."

"How could you let this happen?" she said angrily. "Steve please, where did they take them? Who do I talk to about this foolishness?

"You have to leave Alicia," he said firmly.

As if in a trance Alicia walked back to her suburban. She sat outside the school until dark, waiting for her children to come out the door. She kept thinking "*through no fault of mine, my children are now caught up in the foster system. What more can I do? They are clean and well looked after. Sure we are living in a travel trailer in a parking lot, but this is only temporary. I will find a place to live as soon as I can afford it.*"

"*What is Cliff Walker trying to prove?*" Angrily she slammed her fist against the steering wheel. "*How can I fight him? He has the government backing him and I can barely afford to live.*"

100

What Steve hadn't told her was that the kids refused to go. Randy had finally been dragged away by that Walker fellow. Both of the girls were crying as they followed Randy down the hall. Something about the whole thing felt wrong. He knew Alicia well enough to know how she would react.

Wiping tears from his eyes he put on his jacket and locked his office door. This had been one of the most difficult days of his life. As he drove out of the parking lot he could see Alicia still sitting in her car waiting for her children.

"Where could they be? Who will look after them now?" Sometimes she still had nightmares about the treatment she had received. Her heart ached with grief, what was she going to do now?   She sat there until dark. The lights in the school were turned off and the building was empty.

"Somehow I missed them. They must be at home wondering where I am," she thought.

She raced home. When she drove up to the trailer she saw it was also dark, her children weren't there. Alicia went inside, threw herself on the girl's bed, screaming and sobbing into Erin's pillow until she fell asleep.

The next morning Alicia dragged herself to work. She couldn't afford to lose her job, but when she walked into the staff room she couldn't continue. She put her head on the table and cried.

`Mrs. Browning, do you need help?" a voice asked.

She shook her head no, not trusting herself to speak.

"Alicia what is it?' a male voice inquired.

She looked up to see Al Thompson, the store manager, standing beside her. He had such a kind face and gentle manner when dealing with people. Touching her on the shoulder he said sternly, "Stop crying and tell me what all these tears are about."

"Oh Mr. Thompson I need help. They took my kids away yesterday."

"What do you mean they took your kids away? Who did?"

"Social Services. They were at the school waiting yesterday waiting for me to drop them off. They didn't even have the nerve to come and tell me."

"Alicia," he said kindly, "Come to my office and tell me the whole story. I've noticed you and your children living in the parking lot. I let you stay because you weren't hurting anybody. I figured you were down on your luck."

Once in his office the whole ugly story spilled out of her mouth – how she had lost the acreage, how her bank accounts were seized and why she had lost her job at the school. She told him that Moe had phoned her from Mexico and wasn't planning on coming back. Now her kids were gone too.

"Has anybody tried to help you?"

She shook her head. "I haven't asked," 'she admitted.

"Alicia, go home and take the rest of the day off."

"I have to work. I can't afford to lose my job."

"Never mind that today. I am going to make a couple of calls. Go home and I will stop by later."

Alicia had no sooner got home when there was a knock on the door. Opening it, she saw Cliff Walker standing there. He muscled his way inside.

"Are you ready to talk now? Tell me what I want to know bitch, I know you have been are lying. You are really stupid, do you know that? I have taken your home away. I got you fired from the school, told them you were dealing drugs. I tried to get you fired from here, but that guy wouldn't go for it. Now I have your kids, and there isn't a damn thing you can do. I can keep making your life a living hell if you don't tell me what I want to know. Telling me what you know will make this mess go away."

Suddenly Alicia was mad. "You arrogant SOB. Who the hell do you think you are? I am going to report you for harassment. Get out of here now," she screamed at him shrilly.

`Lady you try whatever you want. I work for the government, and I will get what I want one way or another."

CHAPTER TWELVE

Al Thompson was furious. Something was wrong with her story, He had been watching out for her ever since she moved into the parking lot. He also had security checking on her at night, As far as he could see, someone was taking advantage of her.

Usually he tried not to get involved in all the mini dramas that involved his staff, but this felt different. He literally had to throw the guy out of his office – the government guy who walked in demanding he fire her. Now that he knew her side of the story, he decided to step in. Picking up the phone he placed a call to his brother-in-law Gregg Waring, who was a lawyer.

"Hey Gregg, how's it going. You busy today?"

"Of course Al, you know me, I'm always busy. What can I do for you?"

"Do you think you could spare me an hour? I want you to meet with one of my employees today, name of Alicia Browning."

"Oh Al, tell me you haven't fallen for another sob story - have you?"

"You might say that. This lady has a serious problem and needs a good lawyer right away."

"Can she pay? Usually when you phone you want me to do this for free."

"Don't think so. Guess I am asking you to take on another Pro Bono case. Will you at least listen to her story, and then decide if you can help her?"

"Oh crap, if you weren't my favourite brother-in-law, I would say no and hang up."

"Thanks Gregg I really appreciate you doing this for me. This is what she told me, and then you can decide for yourself if you want to get involved." Al repeated Alicia's story. They arranged to meet at Alicia's trailer in one hour. "Oh, and by the way Gregg, inn case you have forgotten, I am your only brother-in-law."

"Yeah I know." Gregg replied affectionately.

When the two men arrived Alicia was still shaking from her encounter with Cliff Walker. "What are you doing here Mr. Thompson? Is something wrong? Do you need me to come back to work?"

"Alicia, this is my brother-in-law Gregg Waring. He is a lawyer, and I have asked him to listen to your story. I thought you may need some help getting your kids back and all," he replied

Alicia opened the door and invited both men in. "Go ahead Gregg; I need to get back to work."

Gregg walked into the trailer and waited for Alicia to find a place for him to sit.

He looked at her and thought *"Al sure can pick them. Another dumb blond, he really has a thing for them. I'll listen to her story, tell Al I can't help her, and be out of here. Ten minutes tops."*

Alicia was a mess. Her hair was unkempt and sticking out all over. Her eyes were red from crying, her lips cracked from licking them. She had lost twenty pounds since this whole ordeal had started, and her clothes hung on her tiny frame.

Sounding as professional as possible he said, "Mrs. Browning, Al told me you needed a lawyer. Do you mind telling me what is going on?"

Calmly, and without emotion Alicia recounted her story. Gregg listened, and jotted down notes on the note pad he always carried with him. He didn't interrupt her except to have her clarify the few points he was having difficulty understanding.

He was seething with anger. Never, in his days of practising law had he seen a person's right so blatantly violated - that is, if her story was true. Against his better judgement he said "I can't guarantee anything Alicia, but I will make an honest effort to get your kids back to you today."

Numbly Alicia shook her head and whispered "please."

"Stay here until you hear from me. I am going back to my office to see what I can shake up. In the meantime, don't go any place or talk to anyone, and don't let that Cliff Walker fellow back in here."

Gregg went back to Al's office. In a teasing way he said, "You sure know how to pick them, tell me everything you know."

Once he had a full understanding of the story he left. Gregg wondered if he could help her. He didn't know, but this was a challenge he was willing to accept. Nobody deserved that sort of treatment, especially a woman only marginally involved. This could be a full time job for a while; good thing business was slow at the office right now.

Once back in his office, Gregg called Marcie, his secretary, to bring her note pad to take notes. He explained Alicia's plight and what course of action he was going to follow. "I need some phone numbers right away. First, the Drug Enforcement Agency here in town, then Chief Sloan and Judge Harrison. Before I get carried away we need to check out the facts. Find out all you can about her husband Maurice, and that Walker fellow."

His first call was to Tom Sloan, the Chief of Police.

"Tom, Gregg Waring here. I need some information on a Maurice Browning and his wife Alicia. I am representing her as of today."

"Sure Gregg, what do you want to know?"

"First of all, is he in the country, and secondly is the story that she is telling me true?"

"As far as we know Browning got picked up at the border transporting drugs. He is really a nice guy, but got caught up in the lure of big money. He had no idea what he was getting himself into or who he was getting mixed up with. Basically he got in over his head. It's an ugly story. These guys are not only smuggling drugs across the border, they are also involved with human trafficking. We are hoping we can get Browning out of this without him getting hurt.

We figure he slipped back into Mexico while he was out on bail. We had been watching him and a couple other truckers for some time to see if we could nail down who their contacts were. An over exuberant border guard, out to make a name for himself, spoiled our operation for the time being. If Browning got back into Mexico, we can keep track

108

of him. The authorities there are working with us. This is a big operation and we want it shut down."

"You know his wife and family are going through hell. The Drug Enforcement Agency seized her home, her bank accounts, and now she and her kids are living in a trailer in the Waymart parking lot. Some guy by the name of Cliff Walker is doing a real number on her. He went so far as to talk to Steve Wilson and the school board and got her fired. Yesterday, he talked Emily Smith from Social Services into apprehending her kids."

"He is real miserable so and so," replied Chief Sloan, "walks around with a chip on his shoulder. That guy is on a mission to destroy anybody connected with drugs, and he doesn't care who he hurts in the process. The heck of it is, he gets results and has been getting away with this kind of behaviour for years. We told him to take it easy on her for now, but he follows his own agenda."

"Got a number for him?"

By the time Gregg hung up, he had the phone number of Cliff Walker's cell phone. He also had assurances from Chief Sloan that they would keep him informed on all developments of the case.

He placed the call and was surprised to hear Walker answer on the first ring.

"Cliff Walker speaking."

"This is Gregg Waring, legal counsel for Alicia Browning."

"She finally got a lawyer did she?"

"Yes. Can we get together sometime today?"

"I'll be back in my office in about an hour. Meet

me then."

Exactly one hour later, he was sitting across from Cliff Walker. "Can you explain to me what is going on? Mrs. Browning is beside herself with worry. Apparently you convinced Emily Smith to remove her children from school yesterday."

"Sure did. That dumb blond knows more that she is telling me. I am going to find out one way or another who is running the show here in town. I figure Browning will lead us to them sooner or later."

"She claims she doesn't know anything, that her husband kept her out of the loop."

"You believe her? If I keep the kids for a couple more days she will spill her guts."

"And if she doesn't?"

"Guess her kids stay where they are. They'll probably be better off."

Gregg was seething inside. This Cliff Walker had a lousy attitude. He knew he had to be very careful not to let his thoughts show in his voice or on his face

"It sounds to me like you are making this personal?"

"You damn right I am. My nineteen year old brother died from doing drugs. That kid had everything going for him, and now he's dead. I'm out to catch every lousy drug dealer I can get my hands on, and make them pay big time."

"Even if innocent people suffer?"

"I do whatever it takes. She knows, and she will tell me before I am finished."

"Is there any way you could let her kids go and stop holding them hostage. They don't know anything, and they are the ones getting hurt here."

"Tough!"

It was all Gregg could do not to reach across the desk and punch him in the face. Not only did he have a lousy attitude, he had decided to play God. For a man to gloat and be proud of what he had done to this family was more than Gregg could fathom. Unless he fought for her, Alicia didn't stand a chance.

Gregg saw that he wasn't going to get anyplace trying to talk sense into this man. He wasn't going to change his position, no matter what.

After leaving Walker's office, he drove straight to the court house. Instead of phoning Judge Harrison, he was going to take a chance that he was still in his office, and hadn't left for the day. Fortunately, he was still there.

"Gregg, what brings you here so late? I was just leaving."

"Thank you for seeing me sir. I need an injunction to get three kids released from the care of Social Services today."

"This is an unusual request coming from you. I thought you didn't do family law."

"I don't, but these are unusual circumstances."

"This must be serious for you to show up without an appointment." Taking off his coat, he sat down behind his desk and motioned Gregg to sit down on the closest wooden chair. "Tell me what this about, and I will see if there is anything I can do."

Gregg told Judge Harrison about his conversations with Alicia, Cliff Walker and Chief Sloan. "That Walker character is carrying this too far. Browning has been charged, but hasn't been to court yet, never mind being found guilty. At this point we have to assume he is innocent until proven otherwise."

Judge Harrison and Gregg spent the next half hour discussing the legal points of the case. Finally Judge Harrison declared "I am going to grant your injunction. From what you are telling me her rights are being violated, I'll make it valid for a month. I trust you will know what is going on by then, and will keep the court informed. Come back in an hour and the paper work will be ready for you to pick up."

"Thank you Sir, I appreciate this."

"Don't thank me. I am a firm believer that children should be with their parents unless it's proven otherwise."

While he was waiting, Gregg phoned Emily Smith at home. "Emily. I'm in the process of getting an injunction from Judge Harrison for the release of the Browning kids back into their mother's care. I want to pick them up tonight and take them home."

"Won't tomorrow do, I'm tired. This has been a very long day, and besides I have a headache."

They went back and forth, Emily refusing to change her position, Gregg attempting to convince her otherwise.

Finally Gregg said to her "Emily put yourself in this woman's shoes. You have kids. How would you feel if you dropped them off at school one morning knowing they were clean, well fed, and well-dressed although you were in dire circumstances? Then when you go to pick them up after school they aren't there. A crime is said to have been committed, but not proven yet. Someone is blackmailing you by using your position and these kids for the sole purpose of getting information. What would you do?"

"Get a lawyer just as she has, but I can't."

"Why not?"

"That Cliff Walker phoned just before you did, and told me not to release those children tonight. Said he would report me to my supervisor. Said he would make sure I lost my job if I went against him."

"Emily I have an injunction from Judge Harrison. I think you should be more worried about disobeying that."

There was a long silence. "You win Gregg. The kids are at county. I'll go pick them up. Meet you in my office in two hours. I'll have to see the papers first, you understand. I can't release them on just your say so." Then she added, "I'm glad you called. This whole thing hasn't felt right from the beginning, but he had the necessary paper work."

"Deal! Two hours it is."

Gregg was outside the Social Services Building, waiting in his car when she drove up. The five of them went inside to her office. Gregg served her the injunction; she signed the release papers and handed them back to him.

During this time the children hadn't said a word. Gregg could see they were tired, dishevelled and confused. Their eyes were red and swollen from crying. In fact, he was sure they were in shock.

When they were finished, he said to the bewildered children "My name is Gregg, and I am going to take you home to your mother."

He put the two girls into the back seat of his sports car, and Randy in the front with him. They waited until Emily was safely in her car and then drove away.

There was silence until the lights of the Waymart appeared in the distance. Usually not lost for words, Gregg had no idea what to say to these kids. As they saw the lights, the tension in the car began to dissipate. He could hear Sam asking Erin a question, then she said "Mr. Gregg do you know where to go?"

"Sure do little one. I will have you back with your mom in a few minutes."

Within a short time he pulled up to the trailer. "Go see your mom" he told the children. "Tell her I'll be back to see her in the morning." The lights were on, and through the open blinds he could see Alicia huddled in one corner of the couch.

The three kids ran toward the trailer, and then stopped. Erin came walking back and gave Gregg a big hug, "Thank you Mr. Gregg for bringing us home." Then she was gone.

He watched the joyful reunion through the window. It moved him to see the mother and children hugging each other and hearing their joyful laughter.

Alicia gathered her children into her arms. "I

promise you nobody will ever take you away from me again."

Randy said, "That man from the house, he kept asking us questions about dad. Did we know where he was? Who were his friends? Had we ever heard any names when he talked on his cell phone? He wouldn't believe us when we said we didn't know. Is that what he did to you?"

Erin added, "He said he could keep us away from you forever, that we would never see you again. Is that true?"

"Erin I would have found you no matter where you were, and have done everything in my power to get you back. I never would have let you stay there," Alicia declared. "Randy, yes those are the same questions he kept asking me. When I didn't have the answers he wanted he took our house anyway."

"Mommy, I was scared," added Samantha.

Alicia continued comforting the children, convincing them they were safe, and that she would be there in the morning. Randy locked all the doors and closed all the blinds, then double checked the doors before he went to bed.

Although it was crowded, all four of them slept in Alicia's queen size bed. Several times during the night, she felt a small hand reach over and touch her. It was as if each of them needed reassurance that she was there.

CHAPTER THIRTEEN

Alicia lay awake thinking *"All my life, even while Moe and I were married, I have allowed people to walk over me like a doormat. During our marriage I did everything he asked of me, and then some. I was afraid to stand up to him in case he left. After all of that, look at how we have ended up. None of this is my fault, but the kids and I are the ones paying the highest price.*

As if a bolt out of the blue struck her she made a decision. *"Alicia Browning, enough is enough. You deserve better than this. You have three children to look after, and as long as you allow others to be in charge of your life, nothing is going to change. Stop feeling sorry for yourself. You are the only one you can depend upon right now. The time has come to take control of your life, and get the outcomes you want. There is no way in hell you are going to allow anyone to hurt your kids again."*

After giving herself this lecture she immediately began feeling better. Finally she had some direction; she had something to live for. She liked the idea of taking control, but wasn't sure what to do next.

When Gregg returned the next morning a transformation had taken place. The trailer was neat and tidy. All of the newspapers covering the couch had been put into the trash. The dishes were washed and put away. Alicia had showered and pulled her wayward hair into a pony tail. She was wearing a pair of black dress pants, and an attractive lime green sweater that set off her eyes. Gregg could see that she had gone as far as applying a bit of makeup which brightened her face and erased the dark shadows under her eyes. A new aura of confidence and serenity surrounded her.

Gregg's heart leaped in his chest. She was beautiful. He didn't believe in love at first sight, but something was drawing him to her. Maybe it was her vulnerability, her desperation or her insecurity and honesty. Whatever it was had left him tossing and turning all night. He couldn't stop thinking about her. She made him feel like a white knight coming to the rescue of the fair damsel. His gut instinct told him to walk away from this case before he got more involved than he was, but he couldn't.

He didn't want to walk away. An injustice was being committed, and he felt compelled to see this case through to the end. In essence, when he thought back, this was why he became a lawyer in the first place.

"Well kind sir," Alicia said jokingly the next time they met, "where do we go from here?" Then more seriously she added "Gregg I have made up my mind that from now on things are going to be different. None of this is my fault, but my kids and I are paying a heavy price. That stops today. Nobody, and I mean nobody, is ever going to put me in a situation like this again."

"Good girl. I was wondering how long it was

going to take you to get mad and reach this point. Now we can begin to move forward.

I have some plans of my own I have been working on, and want to run the ideas passed you. On Monday morning we will file an application with the courts so you have sole custody of your children. I will talk with Judge Harrison, tell him the situation, and see if he is willing to fast track this through his docket. I am quite sure Moe isn't going to show up to oppose you.

I have asked my secretary to get a copy of the Recovery from Crimes Act and see what rights you do have. I have a feeling that Cliff Walker has, for whatever reason, taken this personally, and overstepped his authority. In the meantime, I want you to think room by room what was in your home, and how long you had it. This includes gifts and things you bought with your own money. Place a mark beside what you have had longer than three years.

I am going to the police station today and try to find out exactly where they are in the process of getting Moe extradited back here."

"On what grounds?"

"Leaving the country while he was on bail."

"I have made some decisions too Gregg. I'm going to get the children settled down, and get counselling for all of us, if I think we need it. I am also going to ask for more hours at work. I have also decided that we are staying here until I can get enough money saved for an apartment."

They sat there for a long time discussing Greg's

plan in detail. Although Alicia didn't understand the process, they had a starting point, and something to work toward.

Life settled into a routine. The school bus picked the children up at eight in the morning and dropped them off at four thirty. By then Alicia was already home from work. She had applied for, and got a full time position as day supervisor. Now she had a medical and dental plan.

She began looking forward to Gregg stopping by every day. Officially, his visits were to keep her up to date on what was happening, unofficially they enjoyed being with each other. His visits made her feel less lonely, although sometimes in the middle of the night, she yearned to have Moe beside her, to hold and make love to her.

Gregg was good with the children and they liked him too. If she had to work on a weekend he gladly volunteered to keep them busy. Sometimes, on Saturday night, he took them all out for a burger and a movie. Mostly though, she and Gregg talked.

Alicia shared with him her emotional upbringing of living in one foster home after another. Gregg regaled her with stories of his college antics or what cases he was working on beside hers. Other times they sat in comfortable silence, watching the small television set which had come with the trailer.

He enjoyed being with her and the children, but kept his feelings to himself. He knew it would be a long time before Alicia was healed enough to have another man in her life, and as her lawyer, he couldn't get involved with his client. Once this was all over, he would see to it that their relationship was different, but until then he would bide his time. First things first.

CHAPTER FOURTEEN

One day Gregg came to the trailer very excited. "Alicia, I have some good news. Judge Harrison has granted you full custody of your children for the next six months."

"Six months? I am their mother for heaven's sake. Six months indeed. I have a notion to call that judge and tell him what I think of that arrangement."

"Alicia. I know that isn't what you expected to hear, but that's the way the court operates. Moe still has to be served the custody papers and be given an opportunity to respond. If he doesn't, then you get permanent custody."

"It doesn't seem fair. Nobody seems to know where he is."

"The fact that Social services apprehended your kids played a big role in Judges Harrison's decision. Basically you have to prove you are a fit mother and can provide for your children. Now, for the second part of my good news, the sheriff's department located Moe in Juarez Mexico. He is running drugs down there as well as delivering them to the truckers who cross the border using the same routine as he did. The Mexican officials are watching him and gathering information. When the time is right, they are hoping to shut down the whole operation. After that they will bring him back here. Plans are going ahead to extradite him back here as soon as he is picked up. They want to get him home without getting hurt. Alicia. I am sorry to have to tell you all of this. I know this isn't the kind of information you want to hear."

Sadly she looked up at him and replied "It's not your fault. Those are the choices he made. Gregg, will we be able to see him when he gets back?"

"Possibly, it will depend upon where he is."

"Gregg, that's not good enough. I will have to know where he is. The children have the right to see their father even if he is in jail. Like it or not, he is their father, and still my husband."

"Alicia, why would you want to put you and the children through that heartbreak again? Your wounds are just beginning to heal. You are getting your life back, and building a new one without him."

"How can I make you understand that deep down Moe is a good man? He loves us and was good to us. I think he just got caught up in the thrill, and then was in way over his head. I will stand by him until he tells me different.

"Do you still love him after all he has put you through?" he asked.

"Yes."

There seemed to be nothing more for Gregg to say. After a few minutes he excused himself and left.

A full week passed before Alicia saw him again. He phoned every evening but kept telling her he was tied up in court on a difficult case which was taking most of his time. Somehow there was a subtle difference in their talks. They weren't as carefree as before. Something had changed.

Then, one day, he suddenly showed up at the trailer again. The coolness in his attitude was gone. He was the old Gregg again.

"Alicia, I finally got a copy of the inventory of the furniture taken from your house.

"Oh, I forgot you had asked me to do that."

"No big deal. Go over this list; mark what you have had more than three years, what you received as gifts from people other than Moe, and what you bought yourself. Once this is done I am going to petition the court to get them back for you. I can't save it all but am going to try and save what I can. I can't stop the process, but I can hold it up until Moe is convicted of a crime."

"Thanks Gregg. I appreciate all you are doing. One thing has been bothering me. How much is this going to cost me? I don't know how I will pay you for the time and effort you have put in, but I will find a way.

"Don't worry your pretty little head about that."

"Don't you ever say that to me again. Moe always used to say that and look where it got me." Alicia snapped at him.

"Whoa girl, I'm sorry. To tell you the truth, I have no idea what this will cost you. I have just been making notes, I haven't had my secretary sit down and figure out the cost or the number of hours yet. I promise you I will let you know when all of the loose ends are wrapped up."

"Promise? I pay my own way, and I don't want to end up owing anybody anything."

"Yeah sure, I promise," said Gregg convincingly. He had no intention of doing so.

"One more thing Alicia, the income tax is snooping around too. Moe filed all of his taxes and legitimate expenses, but he didn't declare any of his extra income. The two departments will have to fight out who gets what between them. This definitely gives us more time."

The days passed quickly with no more news. The children were thriving in their new environment. Alicia was enjoying her work, and she and Gregg were becoming good friends.

On several occasions she noticed a white Ford pickup truck sitting in the parking lot when she got home from work. It was always parked in the same spot, right close to her trailer.

Then one evening, she got a glimpse of the driver. It was Cliff Walker. Her heart jumped into her throat, and that sick uneasy feeling came back into the pit of her stomach.

At first she tried to ignore the fact he was out there sitting in his truck. He would arrive shortly after she got home from work and stay until she turned the lights off in the evening." What more does he want from me?"

Then one evening he made his intentions known. She had sent Randy and Sam to the store to get some milk for breakfast. Much to her dismay, he got out of the truck and approached them on their way back.

Banging the trailer door behind her she stormed over to the truck. Cliff Walker was so engrossed in talking to the children that he didn't see her until she was right in front of him.

"Randy, take Sam home and lock the door. Don't let anyone in unless it's me." Then, turning to Cliff Walker she said, "I told you to never come near me or my kids again. Just what do you think you are accomplishing by sitting here every evening?" she spat at him.

"Like it or not this is a free country, and I can park anywhere I please. This is a public parking lot isn't it?"

"You stay away from us. Haven't you caused enough trouble? You have already taken everything I have, and then some."

"I want your husband."

"Then go find him. Make yourself useful for a change."

Spinning on her heel, head held high, she began to walk away. Cliff Walker's laughter followed her.

Then, she turned around and walked back to him. Looking right into his eyes she said, "If you don't stop, I am going to go to your supervisor and get a restraining order to keep you away from me. Two can play your silly little game."

"You stupid broad, you are crazy if you think that will help. It won't do you any good."

"We will find out won't we?" replied Alicia.

She hoped this would put an end to his harassment, but it didn't. He continued sitting there every evening. When he tried to talk to the kids they ran into the trailer and hid. She was frightened. He was following her. Wherever she went, he was there. She hadn't told Gregg about what was happening because she was sure she could handle the situation.

The last straw occurred when he came to the door and pushed his way inside. "So I hear they found your old man in Juarez Mexico. He is going to be some pissed when he finds out all of his stuff is gone. Have you told him about that yet?"

`You get out of here and leave us alone." Alicia demanded, her voice trembling in fear and rage. "I have told you time and time again, I don't know anything. I haven't heard from him in months."

"Are you really that stupid? Didn't you ask him where the money was coming from? You had to know something was up?"

Alicia replied through clenched teeth, "either you leave us alone, or I will report you to your superiors. Now get out of here."

"You stupid broad, this is part of my job. They know what I am doing, and whatever you do won't stop me."

Alicia slammed the door shut in his face and leaned against it, shaking with anger. Who did he think he was anyway? Picking up the phone she called Gregg, and told him what had just taken place.

"He is still sitting out there. Please can you come over until he leaves? I'm afraid he may hurt us. I know I have made him very angry."

He arrived within ten minutes. Parking his car beside the trailer he walked over to Cliff Walker's truck. Alicia could see they were arguing. Then Cliff got out of his truck, grabbed Gregg by the collar of his jacket, and began screaming right into his face. Gregg swung his fist and hit him in the jaw. Cliff dropped his hands, got into his truck, spinning his tires as he drove away.

When Gregg entered the trailer Alicia looked at him and said gently, "Are you hurt?"

He held out his arms and she threw herself into them. Laying her head against his chest she cried. He held her until the sobbing stopped, then, without thinking, he put his hand under her chin, lifted her face and kissed her softly on the lips.

At first she resisted, then sank into his embrace. Throwing her arms around his neck she kissed him back, her hungry body pressing against him. She felt his manhood rise against her. Then she remembered this wasn't Moe. Abruptly she stopped, and putting her hands on his chest she pushed him away

"Stop Gregg." she said breathlessly. "I'm still married to Moe, I can't do this."

"Alicia I love you. I have from the first time I saw you with those red eyes and that runny nose." He tried to pull her back into his arms.

"Gregg, please don't say anymore. This is impossible. Besides there is no way I will ever again put myself in the position of being controlled by someone, not even you. I need you as my friend right now, more than I need a lover."

Gregg stepped back as if he had been slapped. Is this what she thought, that he was trying to control her?

"Okay from now on it's strictly friends. I promise not to throw myself at you again" he replied, somewhat bitterly.

Alicia smiled sadly. "Promise?"

If circumstances had been different she would have admitted that she loved him too, but Moe stood like a ghost between them. The one man she loved didn't love her, the other did, but she wasn't free to return his love.

The children came bursting into the trailer keeping Gregg busy for the next hour. He teased the girls and wrestled with Randy on the couch. The girls decided three against one made better odds as they tried to wrestle him to the floor. She sat quietly watching them.

Finally Gregg called a halt to the wrestling and put on his jacket. "I think you are safe now. He won't be back. Lock the door behind me, and if he comes back, call the police first, and then me. I don't think he'll bother you anymore."

Back in his car Gregg slapped himself on the side of the head. *"Gregg old boy, you sure blew that. Better tap it cool for a while. It's plain to see she doesn't feel the same way you do. Better give it a rest for now."*

The next morning Alicia followed through on her threat to get a restraining order. The result was Cliff Walker wasn't allowed to come within one half mile of her, the children or her place of residence. A copy of the order was being delivered to his office that same afternoon.

Then she phoned and made an appointment to see Malcolm Smith, Cliff Walker's supervisor. to lodge a formal complaint against him.

"Mrs. Browning. I understand this has been a traumatic time for you. I'll look into this today." he reassured her. "Agent Walker did have the authority to seize your home and property under the Recovery Act."

"I have no doubt about that. But, does that also give him permission to bully me and my children, drag me out of my car, and stalk me while I am in my home? He ridiculed and embarrassed me in front of the other police officers who were at the house. Neither was it necessary for him to have Social services come and take my children as a pressure tactic. Does he even realize how emotionally scarred they are from that ordeal?"

"Mrs. Browning, try and understand. Agent Walker recently lost his youngest brother because of drugs."

"Mr. Smith, he used me. He lied to me. He threatened me by putting his hand on his gun. He terrorized my children. I am sorry he lost his brother, but I am not the criminal here. My husband Moe has not even been convicted of a crime yet. For all we know he may be an innocent bystander himself."

"You are right Mrs. Browning. It is possible that some of Agent Walkers actions have been inappropriate. If you wish, you can lodge a formal complaint or I could bring him in here and talk to him. Either way he will leave you and your children alone."

Alicia thought for a moment. "I intend to lodge a formal complaint. Oh, and by the way, I got a restraining order against him before I came here today. He is to stay one half mile away from me and my children."

"Mrs. Browning isn't it possible you are overreacting a bit. I am sure if I speak to him....."

"No" Alicia interrupted him. "a formal complaint. If you don't want to help me with this then I will go to somebody higher who will."

"Ok if that's the way you want it. My secretary will help you with the complaint forms and you can drop them off signed tomorrow."

As she stood up to leave Mr. Smith said, "Mrs. Browning I am asking you to reconsider. Agent Walker is a good man and an excellent agent. This blot on his record will hold him back for quite some time. He is having an extremely hard time dealing with the loss of his brother. Perhaps he was a little hasty. If you would give him the information he is asking for, I will see what I can do about the whole situation."

"Alicia looked at him with contempt and replied "I will drop those forms off tomorrow." Then turning on her hell she walked out of his office.

CHAPTER FIFTEEN

Although they talked on the phone every second day Alicia avoided being alone with Gregg. When they were together there was a sexual tension neither one wanted to acknowledge. What Gregg didn't know was the mixture of emotions Alicia felt when she was with him. Merely being in his presence made her feel anxious.

One night, early in December, shortly after she had gone to bed, her cell phone rang.

'Hello" she said sleepily *"Who would be calling this time of the night?"*

"Alicia," the voice said.

"Moe. is it really you?" She sat up straight.

"Yeah, baby girl it's me. Wasn't sure if you still had the same number or not. Thought I would take a chance and try anyway. I don't have much time to talk. Are you still there?"

'Yes, I'm here. I can't believe it is really you after so long."

"Thought you might hang up when you heard my voice. Listen to me. Something big is going on here, and I'm not sure what. The first chance I get I'm going to slip back across the border, and come home. This life isn't for me. My life is there with you and the kids."

"You will go to jail."

"I know that, but I will be safer in there than I am here right now. I don't trust these guys very much. I'm going to catch a ride with the next truck out, then turn myself in at the border."

"We will be waiting for you."

"I know."

Then Alicia heard him say to someone in the background. "I'll be right there. Give me a minute."

"Baby girl I love you, more than you will ever know. Tell the kids how much I love them. I am sorry. I can't believe that I did this to you, but when I get home I will make it up to you. I promise. The only reason I came here was to protect you and the kids. Now all I want now is to come, that is if you will have me. This life isn't for me. I'll try to send you some money for the kids Christmas presents. I have a feeling that all of you are having a pretty rough time?"

"Yes Moe, it has been hard, but we can get through anything now knowing that you are on your way home. I love you. Moe, please get here as soon as you can. We miss you, and please try to stay safe."

"Baby girl, please forgive me. I love you so much," then he was gone.

Turning to the other men in the room he said "let's get this over with."

Alicia checked to be sure the phone call had not awakened the children then sat down on the couch, a blanket wrapped around her shoulders. She huddled in the corner, knees pulled up to her chest, arms tucked around her knees. She made no effort to stop the tears running down her cheeks. *"Even if he was going to be in jail, I want him back safely. We will move, start over, whatever is necessary to be a complete family again."*

December was a blur. Alicia worked every available overtime hour she could get. There were school trips and Christmas concerts with Gregg stepping in and helping her out.

Although winter didn't usually get very cold Amanda's husband came over and helped her winterize the trailer. He wrapped heat tapes around the water and sewer lines so they wouldn't freeze and break. He also showed her how to relight the furnace in case she ran out of propane in the middle of the night.

She found a small artificial Christmas tree. It was a foot tall, already decorated with gaudy lime green and purple balls, and clear lights. There was no room on the cupboard, so they hung it upside down over the table. Erin and Sam hung red and silver garland around the windows and mirrors.

She was able to get the children a few presents. The money from Moe never materialized, and she had not heard from him again. Randy wanted an X-Box, but she couldn't afford to get one for him this year.

The first few days after Moe's call she jumped every time a car door slammed thinking that he was finally home. Since his phone call she had felt torn, part of her was anxiously awaiting his return, the other part wasn't sure if she wanted him back in their lives again. There were also her feelings for Gregg to consider.

Her boss, Al Thompson and his wife Clara insisted they celebrate Christmas with them. Of course Gregg was there. He gave the kids roller blades and helmets. She gave him the latest book by his favourite author, and a new brown sweater to replace the ratty one he wore all the time. He gave her a cultured pearl necklace and a gift certificate for a day at the Spa.

Al and his wife both came from large families, and there were people were coming and going all day. This was the first time they had celebrated with such a big family. Usually there was only the five of them.

After supper Gregg drove them home. On the way Randy said sleepily "mom, this has been the best Christmas. I just wish dad was here to share it with us."

"I know Randy, I am sure he is thinking of us no matter where he is. If he could have come he would have."

Gregg listened to this exchange. He wished he was the one Randy was talking about.

After the Christmas rush Alicia took two weeks off. Since the children were out of school she wanted to be home with them. She also put her name on the list for low rental housing. Two more months and she would have enough saved for her first month's rent and the damage deposit.

She had everything planned out. She had the few items that Gregg managed to recover from the seizure and put into storage for her. It wasn't much, but it was a start. Using her employee discount she would be able to get some basic furniture for their apartment. Most of all she was hopeful – a new year, a new beginning.

CHAPTER SIXTEEN

January second was a day Alicia would remember for the rest of her life. The kids were roller blading in the parking lot, and she was trying to find a way to store their gifts in the limited space she had. Hearing a car door slam she looked out the window surprised to see Amanda, in full uniform, walking toward the trailer. Seconds later Gregg pulled up and the kids raced to show him how well they were doing. She smiled to herself, naturally Sam was last.

Opening the door, she greeted Amanda "how good to see you. It's been too long. I just made some fresh coffee. Want some?"

"Alicia, we have word about Moe. I thought you would want to hear the news from a friend."

"Good news I hope," Alicia said as she filled two cups and motioned Amanda to sit down across the table from her. "Is he coming home soon? He phoned before Christmas and said he was going to come home as soon as he could. We have been waiting for him ever since," she chattered nervously."

"Alicia, I don't know how to tell you this, but Moe is dead. The Mexican authorities found a body in the desert three weeks ago, and through finger prints and dental records they finally made an identification. We received official word this morning."

Alicia turned pale, a look of disbelief on her face. She said to Amanda "you are kidding right? If this is a joke, it isn't very funny."

"Alicia I don't know what to say. We were all hoping for a different outcome. Our department is following up, and we are in contact with the Mexican authorities. From what we can gather Moe became a liability when the extradition order was filed. Apparently, they decided he could tell the authorities too much, got worried, and decided this was their best solution. I am so sorry."

Alicia didn't say anything. She cupped her hand over her mouth, and sat staring out the side window.

"He told me he was coming home. I have been waiting for him ever since. I have been so angry with him, and was convinced he was lying to me again. I called him every name in the book, and he was dead all this time. I had a feeling all along it was going to end like this. I have to go outside and tell the children. They need to hear it from me," she said, her voice rising hysterically, "how can I do this to them?"

"Do you want me to stay with you for a while?" asked Amanda.

Alicia shook her head no; tears welling up in her eyes. What she really wanted to do was run outside and scream.

"I phoned Gregg. He is outside telling your children now. Should I tell him to come in?"

Alicia nodded yes. Amanda walked around the

table, gave her a big hug, and then walked outside

Alicia thought to herself. *"Now I am truly alone, and have lost everything. Oh Moe, how did you get yourself into this? I didn't want big fancy things. I only wanted you. We were happy, what happened?"*

Then she covered her face with both hands as heart wrenching sobs wracked her body. She rocked back and forth as if in agony, unable and unwilling to bear the pain in her heart.

She felt rather than heard Gregg come in. He pulled her out from behind the table, wrapped his arms around her and held her tight. Not a word was spoken between them.

After a short period of time, Amanda brought the children into the trailer. They ran to their mother. Alicia knelt down in front of them, gathered them into her arms, and they cried together.

Gregg and Amanda left the little family to their privacy and went outside, both of them wiping tears from their eyes.

"Will she be able to handle this Gregg" Amanda inquired. "She has been through so much."

"I don't know, but I will be here for her. Damn that man. Alicia didn't deserve to have this happen on top of everything else. This really sucks."

"There is more to this story. Somehow Moe managed to contact us and wanted to give himself up. He asked us to help him get out of there. We put a plan into action, and sent an undercover cop as one of the truck drivers for four consecutive days. When he showed up, we were going to bring him home. Only thing is, he never showed up. Now we know why."

"Are you going to tell Alicia?"

"No, we can't yet. Maybe one day in the future we will be able to."

"What about that Cliff Walker guy. Does he know?"

"No, he doesn't know either."

Gathering strength from somewhere deep inside Alicia forced herself to calm down and stop crying. She sat on the couch, Sam on her knee, Randy and Erin on either side of her.

"Mommy, does this mean daddy is never coming home again?"

Not trusting herself to speak, she nodded yes.

"Where is he then?" asked Sam.

"In Mexico stupid" Randy replied. "He is a bad man."

"No, I mean now." she replied.

"He is in heaven Sam. Randy, your dad wasn't a bad man. He was a good man who got mixed up with some bad people. He thought that he could make our lives better at first, and then he couldn't get away. He phoned just before Christmas, and said he was looking for a way to come home. I didn't tell you because I wanted him to be a surprise when he got here. He asked me tell you that he loved you very much, and was sorry that what he had done hurt you. He loved us all very much. He wanted to make sure we knew that."

Erin, who had been quiet until then said, "I really miss him mom. I want my daddy to come home again."

"Me too baby. I miss him too."

Randy and Erin put their heads on Alicia's shoulder, and she wrapped her arms around them. In turn they each put an arm around Sam, and the four of them cried together. With tears running down her face she held her sobbing children until they finally fell asleep Even then she was reluctant to move, they were all she had left.

There wasn't much Alicia could do. She had to wait for the police on both sides of the border to finish their investigations before Moe's body could be returned home. Gregg handled all of the arrangements for her. Her only request was that he be cremated.

One night, many years ago, she and Moe had talked about what they wanted when they passed away. Moe was very definite about being cremated with only a small grave side service. He didn't want a big deal made because he was dead.

It took three weeks for his ashes to return. There seemed to be a lot of red tape and questions to answer. Cliff Walker showed up to inform her that now they would be proceeding with the sale of their acreage. She had also received a call that she was next in line for one of the low rental apartments, but had to request her name be put down to the bottom of the list. She had to use her savings to pay for Moe's funeral.

The morning of the internment was cool and dull. Few people attended the service. Tuk was there, Sally and her husband, Scott Wilson, the principal of the school, Amanda and her husband Joe, and Gregg.

It was a simple affair, but provided Alicia and the children the closure they so desperately needed.

As she was walking back to her suburban Cliff Walker accosted her. "Guess we both lose," he said. "You don't get your property back, and I don't get to catch the drug dealers. This is your fault you know, you're lying got him killed. Hope you are proud of yourself."

"Get away from me" Alicia spat out angrily. "Get the hell out of my life once and for all."

"My pleasure, oh, and by the way, have a good one." With that he turned and walked away whistling. Alicia, seething with rage watched him go. He looked back, waved and kept on walking.

From that day on Alicia walked around in a daze. *"Maybe Cliff Walker was right. Maybe it was her fault that Moe was dead."*

Her boss had given her all the time off she needed. She got up every morning, got the children off to school, and then went back to bed. In the evening she fed them supper, watched them do their homework, and went to bed the same time as they did.

Either Gregg or Amanda stopped by every day. Sometimes she talked to them, but most times she ignored them. After several weeks of this Gregg timed his arrival to coincide with the that of the school bus.

"Here," he said to the kids, "I need to talk with your mother. Here is twenty dollars for each of you. Go to the store, buy some supper, then you can spend the rest on anything you want. I will come and find you when I am finished. I'll make sure and tell your mom where you are."

"Will this help her not be so sad?" Erin asked.

"I hope so little one, I hope so," Gregg replied.

He took their backpacks and watched as they ran to the front door of the store. Then he opened the door and entered the trailer, dropping the backpacks on the table." Alicia we have to talk." he called out.

"Go away. I don't want to talk to you or anybody else. Leave me alone."

"I'm not going anywhere. I'm coming in there."

He walked into the bedroom, walked around to the other side of the bed and lay down beside her. Then he wrapped his arms around her. He felt her stiffen.

"Leave me alone. Get out of here. I don't need your help anymore. If I hadn't listened to you none of this would have happened. Getting the police involved got him killed."

"No. I'm not leaving."

After several minute Alicia turned, put her head on his chest and cried.

"Oh God I miss him" she sobbed. "He was my rock, my life. Without him I don't know what to do, I don't know how to go on from here. Baby girl he used to call me. Gregg, he did the best he could for us. Did I tell you he went to Mexico to protect us? I have a feeling he knew he was going to die that day, and that's why he phoned. I'm sure he was calling to say goodbye. This is so unfair. We loved him. I keep thinking this is all a bad dream, that I am going to wake up and everything will have returned to normal. That isn't going to happen is it? Nothing will ever be the same."

"I know Alicia I know" he said gently patting her on the back. "Your nightmare is over. Moe is not coming back. The life you had with him is over. I understand how much you loved him and miss him. I was married once a long time ago. She was the love of my life, but she drowned on our honeymoon in Hawaii. A rip tide pulled her out of my arms and I couldn't save her. It will take time, but one day you will be able to move on from here"

He held her for a long time letting her cry. His tears ran down his cheeks, mingling with hers.

After she had cried herself out Gregg said gently, "Alicia you have to realize that you can't blame yourself for the thoughts and feelings you had while waiting for him to come home You had no way of knowing that something had happened to him. None of us did. You are a victim. Cliff Walker used you to assuage his own grief as well as set himself up for a promotion. By protecting all of you, Moe proved how much he loved you..

Your children need you. I need you. You are all they have left. The courage you have shown through all of this is an example they can follow the rest of their lives. I love you. I can't imagine the rest of my life without you or your children. When you are ready, I will be here. In the meantime love Moe, grieve for him, and then let him go.

I am going to tell you something you must never repeat. Moe was coming home. He had contacted the local police department, and was going to turn himself in. He was going to name names on both sides of the border. They sent an agent disguised as a truck driver four days in a row but he never showed. He knew the risk he was taking. In the end, it comes down to the fact he loved you and your children, and wanted to be with you."

"Are you telling me the truth? You're not making this up to make me feel better?"

"No Alicia, I am telling you the truth."

They laid there in silence, clinging to each other, offering each other the comfort they both so desperately needed. Finally Gregg said "get dressed. I gave each of the kids' twenty dollars to spend for supper, and on anything they wanted. Maybe we should go check on them, and make sure they haven't tried to buy the store out? Will you come with me?"

Alicia nodded yes. Gregg left the room, and a dishevelled Alicia gathered her clothes and went into the bathroom for a shower.

"Gregg is right. The time has come to get hold of yourself Alicia Browning." she admonished herself. *"Moe wouldn't want you to carry on this way."*

Once dressed, she and Gregg walked to the store hand in hand.

CHAPTER SEVENTEEN

Three weeks later Alicia received a phone call from Tuk. "Don't hang up on me Alicia. I know I am the last person you want to hear from, but could you meet me at my office this afternoon? There is something we need to talk about."

"I could come around two. It's my day off, and it's not like I have anything more important to do." She replied sarcastically.

Seething with anger she asked herself *"What does he want? When I really needed his help and support he turned his back on me. This had better be important."*

Tuk was waiting at the door when she arrived. Sheepishly he ushered her into his office closing the door behind them.

"Can I get you something Alicia?"

"No," she replied curtly.

"Alicia I am so sorry about what happened. I wanted to be there for you. Moe was like one of my own sons. I don't know even where to start or how to explain all of this to you. A few days after that phone call about Moe that Cliff Walker fellow came to see me. He threatened to close me down for dealing in drugs. He was carrying on like a wild man. He told me if I helped you in any way, especially financially, he was going to say Moe was running drugs for me. I didn't have enough guts to stand up to him, and I will regret that the rest of my life. I let all of you down when you needed me the most.

I have dedicated my life to building this business. Moe came to me about two years ago and told me about the offer he had received. I tried to convince him not to get involved, but the lure of easy money and excitement must have been too hard for him to resist. You were under some financial pressure at the time, and my business wasn't doing well. Money was tight. Moe told me who was behind the offer, and I couldn't take a chance on that Walker fellow finding out how much I knew."

"I understand Tuk. I probably would have done the same thing. It doesn't matter now. All we have left is memories," she said sadly.

"That's why I asked you to come down here today. Right after Moe died that lawyer friend of yours, Gregg what's his name, came to see me. He asked if there was anything I could do to help you. Technically, Moe was still working for me when he was killed. When those government guys came in here and took Moe's records, they messed up Janice's filing system. Anyway she was not a happy lady for a long time and was the one who found it."

"Found what?"

"A $250,000 life insurance policy Moe had taken out when he first started working here. He loved you Alicia, and he wanted to be sure you would be looked after if something happened to him."

"$250,000 dollars?"

"We had forgotten about the darn thing until Janice had to rebuild the records in her computer.

The computer had Moe still working for us so it kept taking the premiums off his pay cheque every month. He hadn't collected his last check, nor informed us he had quit, so it continued taking the money off what he had coming. Walker didn't ask for I, and I didn't offer to give it to him."

"So?"

"When we found this policy I phoned that lawyer friend of yours and he went to work."

"I don't understand Tuk. What are you trying to tell me?"

"The insurance was taken out before the Recovery from Crime Act became law. That means the money is exempt from seizure. The insurance company paid out the claim, and to be on the safe side, Gregg got an affidavit from the court stating that the money belonged to you."

Alicia looked at him and said "you have got to be kidding!"

"No, here it is." He handed her a certified cheque for $250,000 made out in her name.

Alicia let out a whoop, jumped out of her chair, ran around the desk and hugged him. She looked at the cheque, and holding it above her head pirouetted around the office with joy.

"Tuk, do you have any idea what this means to us? I can buy a house. We can move out of the trailer and the parking lot and, and ....." Alicia was stumbling over her words she was so excited.

"Go tell your kids Alicia. You guys have been through more than enough this past year. Oh, and Alicia that Gregg guy is in love with you."

"I know. I care for him too, but I'm not ready to have another man in my life just yet"

Alicia was floating on cloud nine when she arrived at the school to pick up her kids. When they were settled in the car she said to them "Look at this! We are rich! Your daddy had an insurance policy to look after us. We can buy a house. Sam, you and Erin can have your own room. Randy I can get you that X-Box you wanted for Christmas."

She passed the cheque around for each of them to look at. Next they went to the bank. All four of them walked in to make the deposit. Alicia kept out one hundred dollars so they could celebrate by going out for supper. Then she phoned and invited Gregg to celebrate with them.

Silently she looked up at the sky and said "thank you Moe. We miss you and will never forget you."

CHAPTER EIGHTEEN

Alicia spent her money wisely. She put fifty thousand away for each of the children for their education and future needs, purchased a good second hand car, and a few pieces of good furniture. The rest she set aside to purchase a new home. She would have a small mortgage, but that wouldn't be a problem for her to handle.

Each weekend, for the next six weeks, she and the children went house hunting. They finally agreed on a green stucco three bedroom bungalow with a garage and finished basement. The girls each had their own room upstairs, Randy wanted his downstairs.

The house was thirty years old and full of character. The yard, filled with rose bushes, flower beds and green grass, was located on a street lined with mature trees. Included in the purchase price were a fairly new stove, fridge, dishwasher, washing machine and dryer. The best part was that their new house was three blocks from the Waymart, the place they affectionately now called home. Alicia could easily walk to and from work. The kids would be able to stay in their old school, and not have to start making new friends. Each of them, in their own way welcomed the newly found stability in their life.

Alicia gave each of the kids' permission to decorate their own room, but had to step in when

Sam wanted hers painted black. Together they repainted the interior, and she had new laminate flooring installed throughout.

She was also surprised by how little the children asked for, and the sense of pride and ownership they demonstrated for their new home. Living in the trailer for the past year had taught each of them they could survive with less, and that they didn't need expensive trappings to make them happy. They simply needed each other.

On moving day Gregg arranged for the furniture he had rescued from the government to be delivered from storage. There wasn't much, a wooden table with four matching chairs, their beds and dressers, a few basic small appliances, and the large china cabinet Mrs. Clarke had given her. The rest of the boxes, filled with odds and ends were put into the garage to be sorted later. When they had moved to their acreage, Moe had bought all new furniture, and that had been sold at the government auction.

The next step was hooking up their trailer to the old suburban one more time and moving it from the parking lot to the driveway of their new home. Once there, all that was left to be moved into the house were their clothes, books and toys.

When the trailer was empty, Alicia marvelled at how they had survived with so few possessions, and in that tiny space for so long.

The final step was to move the contents of the refrigerator and cupboards into the house, and make sure the propane was turned off. Locking the door signified the closing of that chapter of their lives.

She and the kids had once talked about selling the trailer, but instead decided to keep it and use it for camping.

One Sunday afternoon, shortly after they had moved in, the front door bell rang. Sam answered the door, and then came running back into the kitchen with a terrified look on her face.

"Mommy, that man is here. He wants to talk to you."

"What man?"

"The one who scared us at daddy's house."

Alicia went to the front door to find Cliff Walker standing there looking full of him as usual.

"What are you doing here? Aren't you a long way from home?" she said sarcastically.

"Alicia Browning, I have a seizure order for your house, the furnishings, all contents and the funds in your bank account effective immediately." he said, waving an important looking document in her face.

"You do, do you Mr. Walker?"

"I do! You have five minutes to get your kids and get out."

Alicia looked at him with contempt. She wasn't going to let him play his sick little game a second time. Putting her hands on her hips, and drawing herself up to full size, she said defiantly, "I don't think so Mr. Walker, I will fight you. I hope you are prepared to take this to the Supreme Court, because I am not going anywhere, I know my rights, and you don't scare me this time."

"I will have you arrested."

"Go head. Call in your goons. When we get to the

police station we will ask to see Judge Harrison. I am quite sure he will confirm that he issued an affidavit stating that Moe's insurance policy predated your act, and that you have no claim on anything I have. Then I, Mr. Walker., will have you arrested for defying the restraining order which I am sure is still in effect, Now take your little piece of paper and get the hell off of my property, or I will be the one calling the police."

Cliff Walker's face turned dark red. Saliva was seeping out of the corner of his mouth; his hands were balled into fists. He was furious.

"You don't know what you have done - do you? Those drug dealers are still selling drugs and killing decent people like my brother. Your phone calls and visit to the office messed up my promotion. Now I have a discipline mark on my record and am stuck in this hell hole for the next few years. You screwed me and my life good."

Alicia looked at him coldly. "You did that to yourself. Good bye Mr. Walker and, as you once said to me, have a nice life." Then she slammed the door in his face.

He stood glaring at the door for several seconds. This was the first time, in all his years on the force that someone had dared stand up to him. He had to give her credit, she had guts.

Shrugging his shoulders he sauntered back to his car. Although his actions appeared casual, Cliff Walker was a defeated man. His hoped for victory had vanished, and all he felt was a deep sense of failure for not having avenged his brother's death.

Alicia stood at the kitchen window watching him get into his car and drive away. Two arms snaked around her waist, and a face gently nuzzled the side of her neck.

"Alicia Browning, remind me to never cross you. You are one tough lady when you are mad."

Alicia snuggled into Gregg's arms, the back of her head resting against his chest. Her nightmare was finally over. Gregg didn't know it yet, but their future was just beginning.

ABOUT THE AUTHOR

Judy is fulfilling her lifelong dream of being a writer. Retired from the business world, she lives in Grimshaw Alberta with her husband Bob, four children and four grandsons.

You may contact her at jcoates@telusplanet.net

www.ingramcontent.com/pod-product-compliance
Lightning Source LLC
Chambersburg PA
CBHW060419260626
47161CB00005B/1698